CAST OFF

*The Strange Adventures of
Petra De Winter and Bram Broen*

·EVE YOHALEM·

Dial Books
an imprint of Penguin Group (USA) LLC

DIAL BOOKS
Published by the Penguin Group
Penguin Group (USA) LLC
375 Hudson Street, New York, New York 10014

USA/Canada/UK/Ireland/Australia/New Zealand/India/South Africa/China
penguin.com
A Penguin Random House Company

Library of Congress Cataloging-in-Publication Data
Yohalem, Eve.
Cast off : the strange adventures of Petra De Winter and Bram Broen / Eve Yohalem.
pages cm
Summary: Told in their separate voices, twelve-year-olds Petra, who escaped her abusive father's Amsterdam house in 1663, and Bram, a half-Javanese/half-Dutch boy, relate their adventures at sea after Petra stows away and Bram, son of the ship's carpenter, helps her disguise herself as a boy.
ISBN 978-0-525-42856-5 (hardcover)
[1. Seafaring life--Fiction. 2. Sex role--Fiction. 3. Racially mixed people--Fiction.
4. Runaways--Fiction. 5. Child abuse--Fiction. 6. Sea stories.] I. Title.
PZ7.Y7585Cas 2015
[Fic]--dc23   2014034039

Printed in the United States of America
1 3 5 7 9 10 8 6 4 2

Designed by Maya Tatsukawa
Text set in Maxime

To Nick, my co-pilot and safe harbor

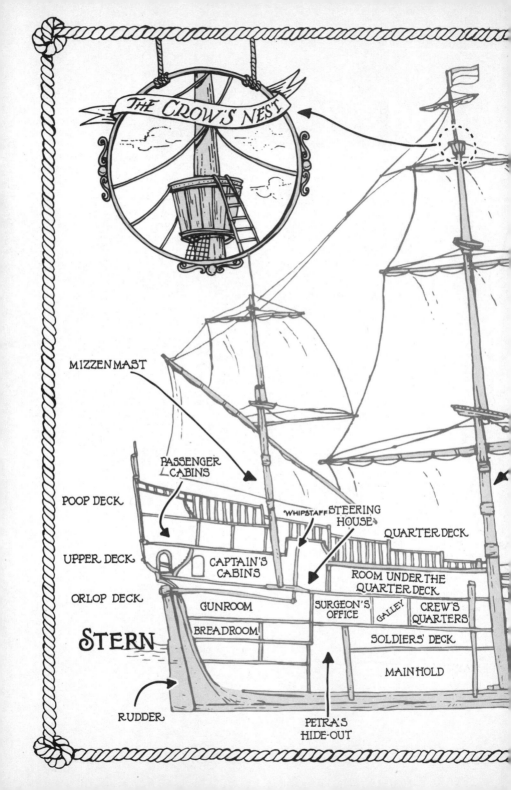

THE CROW'S NEST

MIZZENMAST

PASSENGER CABINS

POOP DECK

WHIPSTAFF STEERING HOUSE

QUARTERDECK

UPPER DECK

CAPTAIN'S CABINS

ROOM UNDER THE QUARTERDECK

ORLOP DECK

GUNROOM

SURGEON'S OFFICE

GALLEY

CREW'S QUARTERS

STERN

BREADROOM

SOLDIERS' DECK

MAIN HOLD

RUDDER

PETRA'S HIDE-OUT

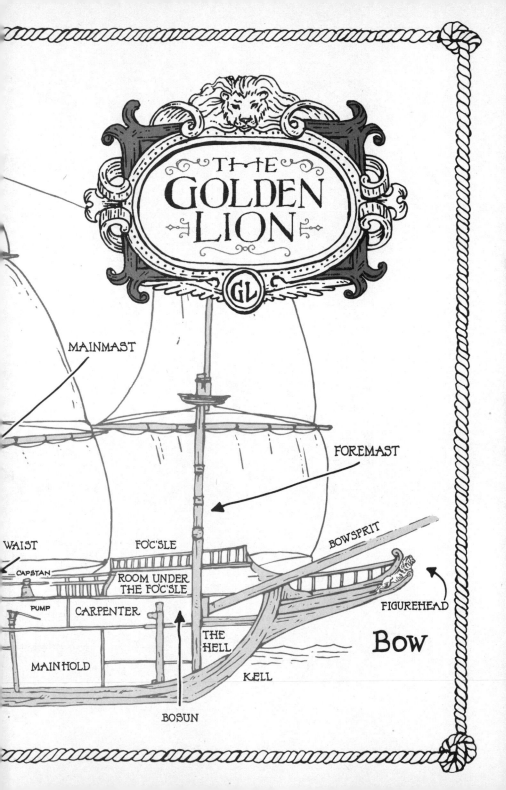

THE
GOLDEN
LION

GL

MAINMAST

FOREMAST

WAIST

FO'C'SLE

BOWSPRIT

CAPSTAN

ROOM UNDER
THE FO'C'SLE

PUMP

CARPENTER

FIGUREHEAD

THE
HELL

Bow

MAINHOLD

KEEL

BOSUN

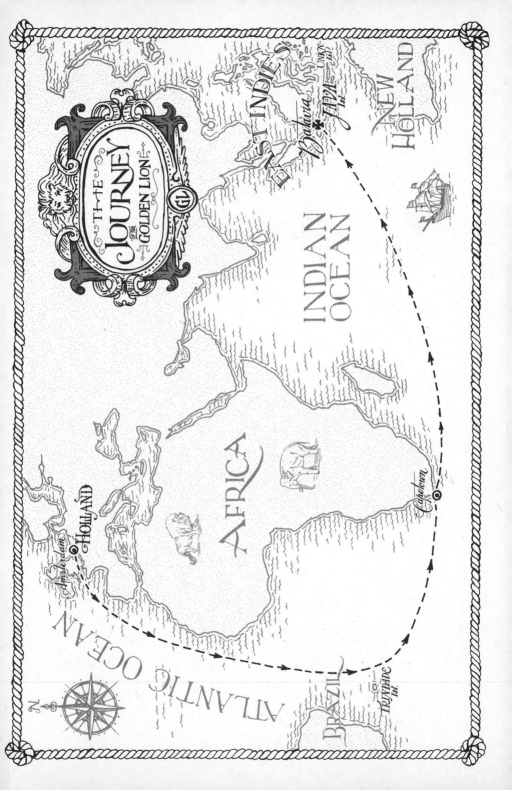

1

April 1663 in the City of Amsterdam

Petra

"Can you fix me up, Miss Petra?"

I paused, knife in the air. Cor, the baker's boy, stood at the kitchen door, gnawing his bottom lip and shuffling from foot to foot. Poor dull Cor. Pocked cheeks, fish eyes, no fat. Needing help today of all days, and still so much to do before Father returned.

"Miss Petra?"

"Show me," I said.

Cor held up his hand, biting his lip. The baker's oven had sucked the flesh from his palm and boiled it.

"Can you fix me?" he asked again.

I could. Human skin is remarkably strong. Albertina says you can pull a needle through it as hard as you like, hard enough to drag a barge off spring mud, and skin won't tear. Nay, it's what's underneath the skin that's most delicate, especially the parts not visible to the human eye. Like the liver. Or the soul.

I looked down at my half-chopped onion, pictured the empty pantry. Albertina was late with the shopping, and we'd never finish dinner on time. Father would be especially hard tonight. He hadn't come home yesterday and his choler was always highest after a night out.

I should tell Cor to go. Let the baker pay for the surgeon.

And see the hand rot and Cor dead of infection before the week was out.

"Come inside," I said, waving him in. "You should try wearing a mitt once in a while."

"I do!" Cor said. "Only I forget sometimes."

Cor and I stood nose to nose though he was two years older than my twelve. He glanced at my cheek. The swelling was gone, but I knew the bruise was still there. It would fade in a day or two, and Father would replace it with another soon enough.

"Sit down," I said, steering Cor to a chair.

"Petje!" Albertina shouldered through the door, her arms weighted with heavy baskets. "Oh Lord! Town was packed. How now, Cor? Burned your hand again?"

She plunked the baskets on the table and a dead chicken spilled out. I set up our medicines next to its head.

"Any bleeding?" Albertina asked.

I held up Cor's hand by the wrist and she squinted at it. "Just blisters," I said.

"What will you use?"

She was testing me out of habit. All of Amsterdam knew our housekeeper had a way with herbs and a needle, and merchants and stable boys alike came to her—and lately me—instead of the surgeon. Our services were free and our healing better.

"Honey and soap to take the fire out, then an oil of rose plaster for the mending," I said, smearing on the first. Cor was trying to be brave, but if he chewed that lip any harder, I'd be stitching it up next.

Albertina dunked the hen into a pot of boiling water in the hearth while I spread the plaster and wrapped Cor's hand in linen.

He left with his usual idiot's grin back in place. But I faced the empty pots and felt the bile drain from my spleen.

"Tina, the time!"

"Don't worry, *mopje,* we'll make it." She put her hands on my shoulders and bent to look into my face. "I promise."

Albertina had been our housekeeper since my parents' marriage, and a mother to me since my own had died five years past. She kissed the top of my head, and I swallowed my fear, choked it down from mouth to throat to chest until an uncracked nut lodged in my belly.

I unpacked hunks of meat, ropes of blood sausage, a

pile of spiny artichokes. Yellow butter sweated in a pewter dish next to a spray of crimson coxcomb flowers. Beneath the table, a leaf of onion paper dirtied the black-and-white checkerboard floor. I snatched it up.

I glanced at the clock on the shelf. Just past four. Father would be home in two hours, but we'd need at least three to make his meal. He'd not stand for lateness. The nut in my belly swelled to a peach stone.

Albertina pulled the chicken from the pot.

"Let me pluck it," I said. "Save your fingers."

She didn't argue. Albertina's knobby old hands were stiff, and she knew I'd finish the job in half the time. I took the bird from her, and she reached for my face, tilted it toward the light.

"Swelling's down," she said, examining my cheek. "The leeches did their work. *Mopje*, I could—"

I jerked my chin away. "We'll never finish in time."

"It won't make a difference if we do or not."

She was right, of course. Nothing helped Father's wretched mood—I had the bruises to prove it.

Albertina set a chair in the doorway, half inside, half out in the afternoon sun.

"Sit," she commanded.

I obeyed, then tucked the bird head-down between my knees and began yanking out its feathers. The cat, Henry Hudson, watched me greedily with one yellow eye and a hollow socket.

I stuffed fistfuls of feathers into a sack, my mind racing over the tasks that would keep Father's anger at bay. He hated mess, and I'd give him no reason to complain. No spot or smear on any window or wall. Everything in its proper place.

And so today I'd changed the bed linens, even though it wasn't Wednesday, polished the silver, scrubbed the floors, scented the drawers with dried lavender. For dinner I'd serve all his favorite foods.

I was such a fool.

While I plucked and worried, Albertina used my knife to chop carrots. She looked up at me without stopping her cutting and grinned around the clay pipe that dangled from her mouth. "The Dutch East India Company fleet's in," she said. "Lord, Petje, you should see them tall ships, all readying themselves to cross the seas. I had to squint my eye to see the tops of the masts. And the sailors! I swear I saw one skip right up just as easy as you and me would stroll through a garden. There must have been thousands, swarming everywhere like ants—all shouting and hollering and hammering and loading. I'll take you to see for yourself tomorrow."

How could she talk of tomorrow when every minute that ticked by brought us closer to failure and fury? But that was Tina. Always urging me to seek out the good bright bits, while I begged her to guard against the dark.

"Perhaps," I said, spitting a chicken feather from my lips.

Tina finished the stew while I laid the dining table in the parlor. A city of porcelain, silver, and linen covered the polished wood—and God's blood if it didn't take half an hour to set it all. I filled Father's glass with wine and mine with small beer and carried in plates of food from the kitchen.

Outside, the church bells rang six o'clock; he'd return any moment now. I dashed through the house, checking for details left undone. I scanned the front room, the many gifts Father had received from grateful traders, trinkets he'd imported from India and Arabia, the French-made spinet I'd never learned to play. Each one dusted and properly placed.

Back to the kitchen, where Albertina swept sawdust from the floor. The stew simmered over a low fire, scenting the air with nutmeg and lemon. I grabbed a rag and scrubbed the table.

"He'll be late," Albertina said, exhaling a bit of smoke around her pipe.

"You can't know that."

Still no sign of him. I ran upstairs to the bedroom Albertina and I shared, where I kicked off my leather slippers and shrugged out of my house robe. Cold air puckered my skin. My black dress, white petticoats, collar, and cuffs I laid on the bed. My linen shift and dirty apron would go into tomorrow's wash.

I took an extra minute to use the chamber pot before

putting on fresh linen and the rest of my clothes and house robe. Crisp folds, spotless bodice. Nothing for him to find fault with here.

In the small mirror on the wall I glimpsed a mess of hay stuffed under a skewed white lawn cap. I untied the cap and whipped a brush through the tangled strands, then pulled my hair tight enough to stretch the corners of my eyes before tying it up again.

With a candlestick in one hand and the chamber pot on my hip, I made my way downstairs, mindful of my sloshy burden. A spider had sewn its web in the corner of the ceiling; a handprint on the landing window glowed in the yellow light. How had I missed them?

Albertina sat in the kitchen, puffing on her pipe. She too had freshened up and wore a clean apron over her good brown dress. I spied a smudge on one of the blue-and-white baseboard tiles.

"Tina, can you get that?" I asked, pointing at the spot with my chin.

Outside, I peered down the street, searching for his dark form, but no one was out. Just rows of tall houses along the canal, each one different, but all with sweeping gables under tiled roofs with columns of tall windows in their brick faces. In front of the painted doors, white stone steps gleamed like tallow wax in the hazy dusk. At first light tomorrow I'd be out here again scrubbing ours like a good Dutch housewife.

I dropped to my knees, emptied the pot into the canal. I was leaning over the muck, holding my breath and trying not to fall in, when I heard the snap of a walking stick on the stone behind me.

"You look like a scullery maid."

"Good evening, Father."

2

Bram

To get the color of blood right, you got to use madder root. It's got the stain of earth but not the heat of cinnabar. You can't use real blood for blood 'cause it goes brown when it dries. I know 'cause I tried.

Making red madder paint takes too much time, so you got to buy it. First there's growing, drying, stripping, and pounding. Then the color-maker cooks the pulp in a barrel for a couple of years. After that he mixes it with some alum and potash powder. Add some oil, and you got paint.

Once, on Java where I'm from, I saw a tiger slink into a rice field and kill a slave boy. Next day, I painted a picture of it. For the blood, I colored the boy's throat with red madder. Let it drip off my brush onto his chest and sarong. I can see that painting like it's right in front of me, even though it's lost six thousand sea miles away on Java. For the tiger's body, I mixed vermilion with lead white to get orange and cut the coat with black charcoal. But 'twas red madder that covered the animal's teeth.

If I was painting the sky tonight, I'd use bone black. When I ask the cook right, he makes it up for me. Holds back a few splinters from a cow's shin or a pig's spine and chars 'em in a tight oven. *Voilà*, as the Frenchies say. Night.

I'd dirty the sky with umber, though, for clouds and mist, and spray it with lead-tin yellow for the lights of Amsterdam pissing into the heavens.

"I'll only be gone a couple of hours, Bram."

Pa and me stood at the bow rail of the *Golden Lion,* far and away the biggest ship in the Amsterdam harbor, looking out at the wharf.

"Don't worry about me," I said. "I'll be fine."

"Take you with me if I could," Pa said.

"I know."

He would, too. But it's against the law for *mestizos*—mixed-race bastards of Dutch fathers and East Indies mothers—to step foot on Dutch soil. And Dutch soil was what we was looking at. Two years back, when Ma died and I'd no family to take me in, the captain said I could come aboard only if Pa swore I'd never leave the ship anywhere north of Africa. Pa don't break promises.

He pulled off my knit cap and rubbed my hair. We wore the same sailor's slops—short baggy trousers, open-collar shirt, short jacket, and neckerchief—and we had the same freckles on our noses, but that was all. His colors was ginger and white, and mine was black and tan.

"Paulus! We're getting old down here," yelled a sailor from a skiff waiting below us.

"Right," Pa said, handing me back my cap. He wasn't one for chitchat.

He climbed over the rail and down the side of the ship for a night out with his mates. I watched 'em steer around other boats moored in the harbor 'til they got to the dock. The ship's figurehead, a gold lion, kept lookout with me.

"What are you looking so happy about?" I said to it. "No legs with a stick up your rump. You're stuck here good as me."

"Come again, Broen?"

First mate Willem Van Plaes slinked up behind me like a skeleton with skin, all bones, with black eyes sunk in deep round holes. His cuffs and collar was fine lace, like he tried to hide his ugliness with fancy bits. Second to the captain and he'd caught me talking to wood animals.

"Beg your pardon, sir, I was—"

"What of my chair, Broen?"

This morning he'd asked me to make him a seat for his cabin. I hadn't started.

"I was just going below to work on it now, sir."

"Good. I expect it finished this evening."

Which meant I'd be up all night. But there'd be no arguing with him. When the cat o' nine tails came out of the bag for whippings, 'twas almost always on Van Plaes's orders.

"As you wish, sir."

He climbed over the rail without sparing me another word, his frilly trimmings flapping in the breeze.

Jeronimo Lobo and little Louis Cheval was next to go. Lobo was Portuguese and a gunner, and Louis was French and looked after the animals. Both was new to the ship.

"We are going out, *Monsieur* Bram! To ze alehouses of Amsterdam for to drink and see ladies. You must come with us!" Excitement—or maybe goat spit—made Louis's straw hair stick up.

"Easy, little Walloon." Lobo hung an arm around the kidkin, gold earbobs flashing. I'd lay five florins the ladies of Amsterdam would be glad to see *him* tonight. That cove had the whitest teeth I'd ever seen. And none missing.

"I told you already, wolf, I am *Français*, not *Walloon*." Louis spit over the rail to make his point.

"My deepest apologies, *Seigneur* Cheval," Lobo said. "Perhaps you will allow me to pay for my insult with a beer."

"*Mais ouis!*" Louis said, cheerly again. "Come with us, *Monsieur* Bram!"

He called me sir, 'though I was only twelve years to his

nine. To Louis I must seem full grown. But which one of us was free to go drinking tonight?

"Leave Broen alone, Louis," Lobo said. "From what I hear, he never leaves the ship."

"Why is that, *monsieur*?"

"Yes, why, Bram? Don't you like our company?" Lobo said.

"Too much to do," I said.

"We *all* 'ave much to do," Louis said to me, then whispered to Lobo, "I think 'ee does not like us."

Louis was wrong, but I couldn't set him straight. I'd have to let him and Lobo think I was some grum ruffian, like the rest of the crew did. I stood there trying not to look as peery as I felt, when Midshipman Johann Majoor came up to us. He was a muscly cove, pink faced and puffed up under his own sway. At fifteen, Majoor was an officer, a job he earned by being born into the right family. Majoor knew the rules about me, even if Louis and Lobo didn't.

"You're not thinking of leaving the ship, are you, Broen?" Majoor said.

"No, sir."

"Good. And I'm afraid I've bad news for you, Lobo," Majoor said. "You need to help load the last of the cargo before you're free tonight. Captain's orders."

Lobo did a decent job of acting like he didn't care, but little Louis's eyes filled with water.

"Come, my man," said Majoor, holding out his hand to Louis, "how'd you like to get drunk with the officers tonight?"

Even if I'd gone with them, I'd still have been alone. To Pa, I was a boy; to Louis, a man. To Midshipman Majoor, I was a drudge. Among the Lions was men from every Christian country, and some heathen lands too, each with his own ugly story.

But out of all the criminals, ex-slave traders, and family run-outs, 'twas me alone who had no place to go.

3

Petra

Albertina waited for us by the open front door.

"*Seigneur* De Winter," she said, using the French title reserved for the wealthy. Albertina knew how to butter his roll. She wouldn't have lasted all these years in our house if she didn't. She took the chamber pot from me and stood at attention, back straight, bosom out, as if she were holding a royal banner and not a bowl meant for catching human soil.

"Albertina," he said, eyeing her from his impressive height.

He hung up his cape, hat, and stick but didn't bother changing his tall boots for buckle shoes. Father had been handsome once, a stern, broad-shouldered man with a full head of black hair that grew past his shoulders. I knew because his marriage portrait hung on the wall where we dined every day. But the red meanness that had always been inside him now showed in the hard set of his thin lips and the glower of his bloodshot eyes.

I inhaled. He smelled like a tavern, of ale and tobacco. His linen collar was stained, his black doublet wrinkled. Despite the cool air, he was sweating.

"Is supper ready?" he asked.

"Yes, Father. Would you like to eat now?"

His reply was to stride past me into the parlor. Tina caught my elbow and gave it a squeeze. My heart squeezed back.

Father sat at the center of the table and glared at his glass while I topped it off with more wine. He downed half of it, then wiped his pointed beard with two fingers.

I sat across from Father while Albertina served us, looking over his shoulder at the wall where his wedding portrait hung, and beside it, the empty space where my mother's had been. He took hers down the week after she died. I'd searched the house from loft to cellar and not been able to find it. He must have sold it. Or thrown it into the canal. I could remember her voice and the softness of her neck, but I'd lost her face.

"Olipodrigo, *seigneur*," Albertina said as she spooned stew onto his plate.

"I can see that."

"Petra wanted to make you a special meal. All your favorite foods."

"Hm," he grunted. He drank the rest of his wine and Albertina refilled his glass. Then she sat down at the table herself.

I breathed in the meaty richness of olipodrigo and the sweet tang of cabbage salad. Hunger pained me, but my stomach wouldn't untwist until Father approved the meal.

As if he could sense my distress, he took his time unfolding his napkin and draping it across his lap. Finally he lifted a piece of meat from the pile on his plate. Hen. He held it in front of his face, examining the flesh and bone. A blob of sauce dripped down his hand and onto the salad, staining the white mound. He sniffed the meat, frowned, and put it into his mouth. His frown deepened into a scowl of disgust.

He spit the mashed-up hen back onto his plate.

"*You call this food?*"

My face burned. Had the stew not cooked long enough?

"Forgive me, Father."

I sneaked the tip of my little finger into the sauce at the edge of my plate. Pretending to wipe away tears, I tasted it. Not raw. Delicious.

"Perhaps if you tried a second bite?" I said, daring to look at him. He scowled even harder at me. "Or another helping. I'll give you mine—"

"You contradict me?"

My fingernails cut my palms. "No, Father."

"Come." He pushed back from the table.

I exchanged a look with Albertina. What choice did I have? I followed Father to the front room, where he paced in front of the fire. On a small table, a Chinese porcelain figurine faced the wrong way. I'd forgotten to turn it. Three laughing pigtailed boys all in a perfect row and one out of line. I yearned to straighten it.

"You've no talent in the kitchen. Let us see if that simple head of yours can remember some basic mathematics. Tell me, girl, when a man invests forty thousand florins in Leiden textiles bound for Java, and the ship founders in the forties, how much money has he lost?"

What madness was this? "Father?"

"How much money has he— *Look at me when I speak to you!*" He grabbed my chin and yanked my face up.

"Forty thousand florins," I squeaked through locked teeth.

"So there is something in that head of yours! Now tell me, if a man invests sixty-five thousand florins in a second ship, this one carrying nutmeg from Banda, if this second ship goes down in a storm, how much money has he lost?"

My jaw throbbed in his grip. Any harder and he'd rip it off my face. "One hundred five thousand florins total, Father."

"Well done!" he thundered. "And now I want you to

truly impress me. If a man invests the remainder of his fortune, *eighty thousand florins,* in a third ship, and this ship is captured by Barbary pirates, *how much has he lost?*"

It was a trick. The answer he wanted wasn't a number, though I'd no better idea. I glanced down. Henry Hudson's yellow eye glinted at me from under a chair. "One hundred—"

"*No!*" He shoved me and I staggered back toward the open fire. "He has *not* lost one hundred eighty-five thousand florins. He has lost everything! *Everything.*" He grabbed my arm and pulled me so close to his face that I could smell his sour breath. "Do you understand me?" He shook me. "Do you?" His spittle sprayed my cheek.

"I believe I—"

"You believe *nothing*! You *know* nothing! *This*"—he let me go and picked up one of the figurines—"is gone." He threw it against the wall, where it shattered. "And *this,*" he said, grabbing an ivory tobacco box and smashing it too. "And *this!*" He spun toward the cabinet and used both hands to push it over. Silver, ivory, porcelain, and glass tumbled from the shelves, and the cabinet crashed on top of the rubble.

"I'm sorry!" I stumbled back, the fire nearly scorching my skirts.

"You are not sorry enough!"

He backhanded my face.

Hot tears blinded me. Oh, he was strong! I ran my

tongue over my lip and tasted blood. Father lunged at me with a raised fist. I threw my arms over my head so my shoulder caught the blow.

"Gone!" he screamed. "All gone!" He whipped around, hands tearing at his hair, his red face a wet mess. I'd seen him in a fury before, but never one like this. *"Gone!"*

This would be no ordinary beating.

He grabbed the poker from the fire and pointed it at me, nostrils flared, chest heaving. I stared at the orange tip, rooted to the ground. His mouth moved but I heard only the rasp of my own breath.

"I've nothing left, you sullen, *stupid, useless—!"*

He drew the poker back, ready to drive it through me. Knuckles white around the handle, arm atremble.

I opened my mouth. The orange tip blurred.

"Nothing!"

I choked. The orange tip plunged.

"Petra!" Albertina screamed.

Her voice unbound me. I ducked, and glowing iron seared the air where I'd stood a moment before. Father staggered, caught his balance, and aimed to swing again. My heart flung itself against my ribs.

"Petje!" Albertina held open the front door.

I jumped over the rubble.

"Go! *Go!"* she urged.

I raced down the red brick walk along the canal, ignoring the few people on our street who gaped at the wild girl

in her leather house slippers. Father wasn't far behind—
the rap of his footsteps spurred me on faster. I sprinted
across a footbridge over the next canal, away from the
lights that spilled from the Indigo Barrel, a favorite alehouse of my father's. I stayed in the shadows, slinking by
the House of Sorrows almshouse until I crossed another
bridge over the next canal into the apple market, empty
now but for a few pieces of rotten fruit. Glancing over my
shoulder, I skidded on a chestnut. Father roared, much
closer than I thought he could be:

"*Petra De Winter!*"

I pressed my back against a stall to catch my breath.
The market was too open. The narrow streets of the old
part of the city would give me better cover. I knew my
way there—until this year when I turned twelve I'd gone
to junior school in an ancient house not far from the Old
Church.

I sprang from the shadows and headed east, past shut-
tered shops with families visible in the windows of the
upper floors. Some of the winding streets were little more
than arm's-length wide. I checked each one to be sure
no one was coming down the other end. For I'd more to
fear than my father. The Night Guard would be on patrol
now that the sun was down. If one of them spotted a girl
running through the streets, they'd catch her and bring
her home.

My feet were silent in their slippers, but I could hear

heavy boots somewhere nearby. The streets were too empty—I could find no place to hide here in the heart of the city. But beyond was the waterfront, swarming with sailors but also full of dark corners where I could stay until Amsterdam's ten o'clock curfew and then make my escape into the black night. I turned north.

Just ahead was the Dam, a big square with the New Church on one side and the half-built Town Hall on another. From there I could see boats in the Amsterdam harbor.

"Petra!" Father shouted.

He sounded near. I darted right, into a dark lane lit only by red lamps above the doors of the houses.

"Hey, girlie, you looking for a job?"

A woman with a powdered face and a black patch shaped like a heart pasted next to her eye leered at me from a doorway.

"No, I—"

An arm slipped around my shoulders. "What's a little miss like you doing so far from home?" said the sailor whose arm it was.

"Let go!"

I'd stumbled upon a part of the city Albertina had never let me visit, and now I understood why. I threw off the arm and ducked away, doubling back the way I'd come, and ran full speed all the way to the waterfront.

Everywhere I looked, casks and crates were stacked high,

each marked with the name of its ship. Boats filled the harbor, their silver masts spiking the night sky like quills on a porcupine's back. A long row of gangplanks lined the pier. Sailors sprang easily down the wobbly boards, laughing. Others milled around the cargo, chatting while they kept guard. The air smelled of wood smoke, tar, salt water, and bilge. I made for the nearest tower of boxes.

A strong hand grasped a hunk of my hair.

4

Bram

The *Lion* was hushed as she ever gets, what with 'most all hands being ashore. Later tonight, two hundred drunk sailors would come back singing. If I was lucky, Pa'd remember to bring me a beer.

I headed down the hatch to the carpenter's cabin, which was where Pa and me bunked, him as ship's carpenter, me as mate. Sometimes we worked in the room under the quarterdeck with the sailmaker, the smith, the cooper, and the other tradesmen who needed room to do their jobs. But there was enough space in our own cabin for small stuff. Our lockers was filled with tools, nails, and the like. We was well stored.

The first time I saw Pa's digs, I thought maybe he was a

criminal and this was his cell. Growing up on an island like Java, sky, air, and water was as natural to me as breathing. Only prisoners lived in the dark with the stink of tallow wax and men who never took a bath. Now I knew Pa and me was lucky. Being head carpenter's an important job on a ship. 'Twas just us in the cabin.

The ceiling below decks was so low, tall men had to stoop. Me, I could stand straight, but maybe not one day. 'Twas dark in the cabin with just the porthole open and night coming on. I lit a lantern. Sniffed. Tallow wax.

I shook myself like a dog. Bleed and wound me if I was going to moon around just 'cause all the other coves was out and about. I took a pencil from my pocket and spread a scrap of brown paper on a sea chest. Made a quick sketch: three legs, a sturdy seat, and a short back.

It'd do.

Pa never drew things before he made 'em. Instead, he screwed up his face like he tasted sour beer and stood rubbing his chin until he worked the thing out in his head. But I drew everything first. That's when it turned real. On the paper.

'Twas a simple chair, just a stool with a back, but I rounded the legs and used the side of my pencil to shade it 'til it looked like life. After I built it, the chair would spend the rest of its days under Van Plaes's rear end. So while I could, I perched an albatross on its back. Wings spread.

I saw one once, up close. An albatross. The thing to

know about those animals is they can fly two hundred leagues in a day without flapping a wing. Just riding the currents from winds and waves. Spread full out, their wings span the length of two tall men head to head, maybe twelve feet in all. When they get hungry, the birds pull those wings in tight and dive straight down like a harpoon to spear prey.

Albatrosses go to land to breed, but they don't stay there long 'cause they need ocean breezes to fly. And you never see 'em past the equator 'cause the currents aren't right up there. They always travel alone, and they like to follow ships. It's good luck to see one—they say albatrosses hold the souls of dead sailors.

On our way here from Batavia, this one bird, he followed us all the way from Cape Hope to Cape Verde. Flake-white body, wings like they was dipped in ink. The whole time we was in the Roaring Forties—twenty-foot waves knocking the *Lion* like she was no more than a skiff—this albatross floated behind us with nary a bump. But when we got up near Verde, we hit the doldrums. Not a breath of wind. And the albatross was as good as beached. He sat on the water like a duck on a pond, and so did the *Lion*.

After a week of going nowhere, things was getting a little close on board. Men was bored. Men was sick of eating fish. Everybody knew 'twas bad luck to kill an albatross, but Dirck Wiggernick shot him anyway.

He shot him with an arrow through the neck. The albatross just tipped over, right in the water. Didn't sink, didn't bleed. Just tipped onto his side. Captain ordered Wiggernick put in chains and the bird fished out for funeral.

The mighty bird didn't look so mighty lying on the deck with his long wings half spread and crooked. His little black eyes staring at nothing. I stared at the arrow in his gullet and my own throat closed up so I could hardly breathe. He looked like nothing more than a big fat goose.

The albatross can go anyplace in the world, so long as he sticks to the ocean. But if he stays too long on land or he flies too far north, he's a dead duck.

As for Wiggernick, he died a few weeks later when the wounds from his whipping festered. But then, so do most people.

5

Petra

"Hush!" Father said when I cried out.

His hands slid to my shoulders, weighing me down while he leaned on me, catching his breath. I opened and closed my mouth like a fish, my eyes stretched lidless.

"Stop. Please. Forgive me." Guilt had hold of him now. Thickening his throat. Pumping up tears. It often went this way. Sooner or later, remorse would follow rage. My battered shoulder throbbed under his weight. I blinked back my own tears. "I'm ruined, Petje," he wept. "Do you see that?"

Oh, I did. He meant penniless. But I felt the sting of my split lip, the ache of the old bruise on my cheek and the fresh one from tonight. I thought of the nights he'd stayed out, pictured the red meanness in his eyes, the hardness of his mouth.

Ruined.

I dropped to my knees.

Father lost his balance, and before he had a chance to reach for me, I was up and running around clusters of cargo. I circled barrels of herring and leaped behind a tower of crates marked ENGLISH CLOTH. I could hear him stumbling after me—it had taken him no time to get back on his feet—and then—

"Pardon me, sir. Have you seen a young girl?"

Before long he'd have every sailor on the quay searching for me! I squeezed between two tall stacks.

"About this tall. Yellow hair. Her mother will be so worried."

I had to move; my nook was open to view. I considered dropping over the side of the dock and hanging from one of the gangplanks, but my strength wouldn't last, and I didn't know how to swim.

Every box and barrel would be full. I'd nowhere to go.

"Pardon me, sir, have you seen . . ."

He was close now. Soon he would round the corner of my hiding place.

"Hoay, mates!" boomed a voice loud enough to carry over gale winds. "Anyone seen a little girl?"

"A little girl? Not unless you want to count Georgius here!" A chorus of laughter.

Ahead was a large bulky shape covered in sailcloth. I launched myself from my shelter, out into open space.

"Hey there, mate. What's that?"

I froze. Torches bobbed along the wharf, carried by sailors searching for me.

"Not the girl. Just a pile o' rope."

I took off again.

I crouched with my back against the sailcloth, panting. Grasped the bottom of the cloth and ducked under it.

Inside, it was pitch-black and warm, and it smelled of . . . *bird*? I cautiously reached out my hands and found metal bars. The cloth must cover cages with—

"*Ow!*"

Something had bitten my finger. I stuck it in my mouth and sucked on it. The beak had been big. A goose, most likely. So like a goose to bite whatever comes its way. A chicken would have gone for my toes.

I used my foot to explore the space around the cages. They seemed to be stacked on a pallet a few inches off the ground. I stepped onto the pallet to keep my feet from view.

"Look sharp, then, Lobo," said a gravel-voiced sailor close by. "We just got this lot to get on board and we're done for the night. I still got a few coins in my pocket and I mean to spend 'em."

He couldn't mean *this* lot, could he? Were sailors about to load the birds onto a ship—and me with them?

There was no way out without being seen—and given over to Father. But to stay meant *boarding a ship.* A ship where I'd no right to be, where the captain, should I be discovered as a stowaway, was perfectly within his rights to toss me overboard.

There was a small hole in the cloth, just below my eye. I hooked in two fingers and tore it a little bigger. If I hunched down, I could see two sailors, one old and one young, the old one a solid slab of oak with gnarled bark for skin, his young friend a shiny, slippery eel, tawny and black with rings of gold in his pierced ears.

"You say you made two East Indies passages with the captain?" the eel asked. He spoke good Dutch with an accent, a soft drawl that sounded of slow afternoons in the Mediterranean sun. Not French. Italian, perhaps, or Portuguese.

"Aye, that I did," said the gravel-voiced oak.

"What do you make of the man?"

"Well, Lobo, let me ask you this." The oak put his arm around his young mate. "You like yer gin?"

"Does a pig like his slops?"

"You mind watching your language?"

A laugh. "Hell, yes!"

"How about enjoyin' the company of a woman in yer bunk?"

"You can be sure of that, *amigo.*" Lobo grinned, revealing perfect white teeth in a brown face.

"Well then, you won't be too fond of our Captain De Ridder."

"He's strict, is he? Runs a tight ship?"

"Tight as a witch's rump."

Lobo looked disappointed. Then he pointed across the wharf. "What's all that noise, Piet? The soldiers loading heavy trunks and twice as many to watch them do it?"

"Those trunks over there?" Piet squinted in the dim light. "The ones marked LION and bound with lead?"

"Aye."

"Those would be the trunks we ain't supposed to know about, seeing as how they contain the payroll of our fine employer, the Dutch East India Company. Three million florins."

"Three million—"

"Gold, silver, and copper, mate. And every coin and bar stamped with the Company seal: *V-O-C,*" said Piet. "But don't you mind about it. Don't matter none if you're here with the birds or over there with one of them trunks strapped to your back. Them payroll boxes won't open for nothing and no one 'til we get to Batavia. You won't get even a quick look-see at them coins and bars. Not even a whiff o' their dust."

"Pardon me, gentlemen. I'm looking for a lost child. My daughter. Have you seen her?"

I held my breath and shrank back to the other side of the

pallet, as far from that voice as I could get in the small space.

"She's a youngster, no taller than this. Yellow hair? I don't know how I could have lost her. I need her back most urgently."

Would Piet and Lobo mistake the anger in Father's voice for worry? A sharp pain pierced my big toe. *Chickens!* I bit my lip to keep from crying out, but the chicken squawked and flapped its wings. Its misery was contagious. The other birds honked and threw their bodies against the cages.

"Quiet in the hold there or I'll wring every one of your necks, the captain's table be damned!" shouted the old sailor called Piet. "Sorry, *seigneur,* we haven't seen your daughter." Piet banged on a cage, which only vexed the birds more. "But we'll keep a sharp lookout for her, I promise you."

There was a long pause during which the birds settled down. I could almost hear Father thinking.

"You're quite certain you haven't seen her?"

"Absolutely, *seigneur,*" said Piet. "We been here all night loading stores."

"What about this cargo here? Might she be under the sailcloth?"

"I don't think so, *seigneur.* It's just chickens and geese under there. But you're welcome to have a look."

"Thank you. I shall."

Sweat ran between my shoulder blades. My tongue went numb. I could scarcely breathe as one side of the sailcloth was flung up and draped over the top of the cages. It was, fortunately, the opposite side from where I crouched. I peeked through the bars at the three men. Piet and Lobo, their faces a matched set of polite concern, and Father, dry eyes, furrowed brow. Clenched fists.

As soon as the air hit them, the birds squawked and beat their wings again.

"You see, *seigneur,* nothing but birds!"

The sailors dropped the cloth.

"Purse-proud goat walks away without even a thank-you," said Lobo.

"Enough yapping, mate. Let's get this stowed before the taverns close."

Now was the moment to slip away. To find a new hiding spot, and another one after that if need be, until it was safe to sneak out of the harbor. In the morning I'd flee the city and walk from village to village offering my services as a maid. Surely some farmer needed an extra pair of hands. Even an orphanage would be better than returning to Father's house, where it was only a matter of time before his rage got the better of his self-control.

"You got your end, mate? Ready now . . . hold fast!"

Forsooth, wherever I went would be less comfortable than my childhood home, and I would miss Albertina every day. Like as not, the farmer or the orphan-master would be just as cruel as Father, and what with hard work and little food, I'd be trading a quick death for a slow one.

Instead, I wrapped my arms around the cages and hung on tight.

6

Petra

"Heave ho!"

The sailors Piet and Lobo lifted the pallet with me on it and moved toward the wharf's edge. All the while, the hideous goose gnawed my knuckles. I ground my teeth and ran through recipes in my mind: orange goose, goose with pistachios, stuffed goose with prunes.

"Oh, misery is the lot of man!" sang Piet.

"Oh, misery man," sang Lobo.

"He drinks his gin whenever he can!"

"Oh, misery man."

My arms ached. The ropes around the stacks dug into my belly. The goose grew tired of my knuckles and moved on to my hair.

The pallet stopped.

"Steady now, mate, lay her down easy," Piet said.

The cloth had slipped a few inches, and I couldn't see out the hole. I heard water slapping against pilings, the scrape of oars against wood, a shoe landing heavily in a boat. I determined that their ship was moored out in the harbor and we were about to row to it.

"On three. One . . . two . . ."

The pallet wobbled in a nauseating fashion and the birds squawked and flapped. I couldn't blame them. Somewhere deep in their birdie brains they must have known they were headed for the pot. Was I as well?

"Handsomely, there! Steady as you go!" Piet urged. "You want we should load 'em one by one?"

"I have it," grunted Lobo. "Just give me a minute."

Stuck in the black, I held my breath while the sailors found their balance and got the boat under way. I fumbled with the sailcloth. Where was that hole?

"Mind the buoy," Piet murmured.

"You're worse than my old grandmother, you know that?"

"I'm just sayin', a young newbie like you, you might miss—"

"I may be but sixteen years and new to the *Lion*, Piet, but trust me, *amigo*, I've eyes like a fat hawk."

"Easy now, hawk," Piet said. "Bring her under the mizzenmast."

I found the hole. Through it I could see Lobo's back and the side of a ship, blackened with tar.

"Hoay, O'Brian! You ready for us?" Piet called.

"Ready and waiting on you, mate, since two bells," answered a boyish voice from above. "Where you been? The taverns—"

"I ain't been dogging it, if that's what you mean to say. Heave her over, mate!"

A heavy rope landed in the boat, followed by a lot of jostling and orders from Piet as he and Lobo tied the pallet to some kind of pulley.

"It's made!" Piet called out. "Hoist away!"

The pallet jerked up and hovered. For a long, sickening moment, it tilted heavily to one side, and only the ropes around the sailcloth kept me from sliding out. If I'd had any dinner, it would have baptized Piet and Lobo.

"Piet!" the sailor O'Brian shouted. "D'you let the newbie stow this lot?"

I realized it was my weight that had unbalanced the load. Quickly, I jammed myself between the two middle stacks of cages.

"Nothing wrong with our stowin', mate. Must be your rigging," Piet shouted back.

Level now, the pallet rose, and me with it, slow and unsteady. I was wedged so tightly I couldn't take a full breath. The birds shrieked and flapped. Minutes crawled by and we climbed higher, until finally we swung hard over.

"Ease her down nicely now," O'Brian said to another sailor.

The pallet thudded heavily onto the deck of the *Lion,* and O'Brian and the other sailor untied it from the pulley. Would they remove the sailcloth too? Had I been chewed and pecked and risked breaking my neck only to be sent back to Father?

The cloth began to slip off.

"Leave it, mate," O'Brian said to his companion. "Them biddies is already in a fit."

I listened to the sound of their footsteps fade before I wriggled out from the cages and lifted the sailcloth over my head.

Oh.

Below, a harbor full of boats rocked in the water, aglow by their lanterns, whilst above, the *Lion's* three masts stretched until their tops vanished into the dark sky. Ropes webbed the whole of the ship, and her sails were tightly rolled, ready to unfurl at the captain's command. From my place at the highest point at the very back of the ship, I could see deck upon deck upon deck laid out before me, five in all. Even I knew a vessel this size was no local cat ship meant to ferry Delft cheese to Rotterdam. Nor a frigate carrying goods to ports in Hamburg and Bruges. Nay, this great ship was headed across oceans and around continents to one of dozens of ports in the Indies and beyond.

She'd be gone for years.

7

Petra

I needed a place to hide forthwith.

I ran down the decks toward the front of the ship and opened the first hatch I saw. Finding no one, I climbed down the ladder into a large cabin strung with hammocks. Cannons lined the outside walls and small sea chests covered the floors. No place for me here. A door at the end of the room led to a cabin that must have belonged to the carpenter—pieces of wood, tools, and sawdust were strewn about. It looked as though someone had left mid-task and could return any moment. Unwise to stay, then. I pressed my ear to the door at the far end of the cabin. Hearing nothing, I lifted the latch and went inside.

This cabin had a bunk built into one wall and a porthole

in another. A storage locker and a seaman's chest nearly filled the space. Whoever lived here was good with a whittling knife. Some dice and a little whale lay on the bed.

Footsteps behind me and the scrape of a chair. The carpenter had returned, and me with no way out, nothing to hide under, nowhere to go. I was too big for the seaman's chest, and, even if I could fit through the porthole, I'd no wish to drown.

That left the storage locker. I lifted the top and found it half full of neatly coiled rope. I looked down at my quilted robe, my layers of skirts and petticoats. Was there room enough?

I lowered myself on top of the rope and pulled my legs into the locker. It was like sitting on a bed of hairy snakes. Even through all my clothes, I felt the prick of sharp fibers. But I'd have to live with the itch if I was to live at all. I stuffed my skirts around my legs, wedging them into corners. Tucked in tight, I couldn't move my legs more than an inch or two.

I lay down and closed the top of the locker, shutting out even the merest scrap of light. My head and feet just touched the ends; my nose was perhaps three inches from the lid.

It was like being buried alive.

I waited, listening for footsteps, for the opening of a door. My heart grew louder and louder until I could feel it beating in my ears.

My chest grew tight. I couldn't take a full breath. I panted small quick puffs of hot air. I had to get out!

But just as I pressed my hands on the lid, I heard voices. I froze. Suddenly the prospect of hiding on a pile of rope in a storage locker didn't seem as bad as the prospect of being found.

I lifted the lid an inch and wadded a corner of my robe in the crack to let in some air. Out of the corner of my eye I could even see the porthole.

The voices were singing.

The locker might do for a short while, but I couldn't stay here for the journey. Whoever lived in this cabin would want his rope, and I'd want things like food and water.

Food. When had I last eaten? Some bread and cheese for a midday meal. My stomach groaned loud enough to be heard in the cabin, had anyone been there.

I yawned. The voices were growing fainter. When they faded altogether, I'd find a better place to hide.

⟡

I slept.

How could I have slept? I slept through the dark, quiet portion of the night when I might have saved myself from starvation or discovery, and woke when it was light and what sounded like a thousand men were hammering every inch of the ship.

A thousand men or no, I couldn't ignore my bladder a minute longer. The sailor who lived in this cabin had come and gone. Perhaps I could do the same.

I climbed out of the locker and made use of my host's slop bucket, emptying the contents out the porthole. Then I pressed my ear to the door. Not a sound. Cracked it open—and found a red-haired man with his back to me tying on a belt strung with tools. No way out now.

I peeled my sweat-sticky shift from my back, eyed the locker with dread.

It occurred to me that were I a twelve-year-old boy instead of a twelve-year-old girl, I could simply lie about being an orphan and join the ship as crew. Instead, I sealed myself away again and waited for night to fall.

8

Bram

"Looks nice and smooth, Pa."

'Twas morning and we was in our cabin, me cutting legs and Pa sanding the frame for a new grindstone for the gunroom—the old one got busted the night before when the midshipmen played at bowling with cannonballs and handspikes. Pa'd polished the same spot for so long, I started to think there'd be nothing left to hold the stone.

"Pa?"

"Hmm?" he answered. A curl of pinewood was stuck in his red hair. It looked like a horn, but I didn't think he'd appreciate me saying it.

"Everything all right?"

He stopped and looked at me. "Sit down, son."

I pulled up a chair, and he pulled up another.

"There's something you should know."

In my experience, nothing good ever came after those words. "Your papa's leaving." "Your ma is dead." "*Mestizos* stay on the ship." What now?

"Last time we was in Amsterdam, I applied for a certificate of legitimacy for you."

"A certificate—?"

"Certificate of legitimacy. If it passes, you'll be legally known as my son. You'd be Dutch."

You'd be Dutch. Hope caught fire in me. With this certificate, I could walk the streets of Amsterdam. I could get married. Own a house. I'd be *free*. 'Twas the first time good news had come after those words. So why did Pa look like there was bad news coming?

"There's more, isn't there?"

"Saw the lawyer last night. We got turned down."

So much for hope.

"But there may be something we can do."

"What's that, Pa?" I was asking 'cause I knew he wanted me to, not because I thought anything we did would make a difference, 'cause I didn't.

"The lawyer—Boone's his name—he said we can try again, and if we got a letter from someone important to the VOC, it would maybe carry weight with the courts."

"What kind of letter?"

"One that says this important fellow knows us and

thinks it's a good idea for you to be my lawful son."

"You have someone in mind?"

"Aye. Captain De Ridder."

Just like I thought. Pa was going to ask for help from the cove who hadn't said a word to me since "Make sure you don't get off this ship north of Africa." I wasn't even sure he knew my name.

"You think he'll say yes?" I asked.

"Not if we ask him now, no," Pa admitted. "You'll have to prove yourself to him, Brammetje. Do the work of two men, day and night. You do that and he'll write the letter."

I wasn't so sure Pa was right, but that hope was still in me. So small I could hardly feel it, but there. If work was the only way to fan that flame, I'd work.

I started in right off. Me and Pa finished the frame, and then I delivered the chair I'd stayed up all night for to Van Plaes. After that I stocked the room under the fo'c'sle with wood, going down to the hold and carrying up each load on my back. Truth told, I felt pretty done in by then, but 'twas only midday and there was repairs to be made to the bilge pump. On my way back up from that, I ran into the sword keep and asked him if any of his blades needed sharpening. He was only too glad to let me at 'em while he had his midday meal with his mates. I ate my codfish and beans in between swipes of the whetstone.

We was set to sail at first light on the morrow, and the *Lion* had to be shipshape by then. I touched up paintwork on her transom where De Ridder could see me do it, stripping off the chipped stuff and freshening it with new 'til dark fell.

Pa went with his mates again for a last night out, and I tidied up the cabin and had gin and leftovers for supper. I needed cordage to tie bundles of staves for the cooper, but I didn't want to go back down to the hold for it. The bosun kept plenty in his locker, though, and I knew he wouldn't mind me taking some if I put it back on the morrow.

The bosun's cabin was next to ours, and his locker was set against the bulkhead. I put my lantern on the floor and opened the lid.

Inside was a girl.

9

Bram

In my experience, boxes sometimes got things inside 'em they shouldn't. I opened a salt pork cask once and found maggots. Found a scorpion inside a jar of nails and five stuiver coins in a fish's belly. But I never found a girl in a storage locker, dead or alive. This one was alive.

And rich, by the look of her. She had on more clothes than a seaman's got in his whole chest. I held up the lantern. Leather slippers too.

She stared at me. I stared at her.

She looked about my age. Yellow hair, blue eyes the color of water, a triangle face. The locker fit her so close 'twas like it was made to hold her.

I'd bet a month's rations the bosun didn't know anything about this girl in his cabin. So who prances around a Dutch East Indiaman in leather slippers hiding in lockers? A rich girl on a lark, that's who. She had to be the daughter of some high-up VOC cove, heart all aflutter over her first big out-and-about. Her ma and pa's gone ashore and she sneaks off to see how the sailors slum it down below. Then she hears some noise or other, gets white-livered and ducks.

Here we go, then.

I stuck out my hand. "Can I help you up, miss?"

"I—" She let the word hang like she couldn't find another to hook to it.

"Would you like help getting out of this storage locker and finding the way to your cabin?"

She sat up then and cleared her throat. "Good evening, sailor," she said in the voice rich girls save for talking down to *mestizos*. "Thank you for your offer, but I've no need of assistance."

Good. "As you wish, miss."

She climbed out of the box and stood there looking fore toward the bow of the ship, when her cabin was sure to be aft, at the stern near the officers' digs. She'd be in one of the fancy passenger berths with a proper bed, not like the hammocks us crew slept in.

"Miss? Your cabin's the other way."

"Of course. I must have got turned around momentarily, er, somehow." Her eyes hopped around the room like a nervy cat. Something was off about her, I just couldn't work out what.

But it didn't matter, 'cause the girl went aft like she should. Or she started to, at any rate. I followed her into my digs, but when she got to the door that went to the crew's quarters, she stopped and grabbed the frame. Her shoulders shook.

Crying. What next?

"You *are* a passenger, aren't you, miss?" I asked.

"Not exactly." She picked her head up and stared at the ceiling.

"Why are you here, then?"

Slowly, she turned around to look at me. "I've nowhere else to go."

In my experience, girls with ten layers of clothes and gold crosses around their necks generally have homes to go to. "There must be someplace. Some family that misses you."

The girl lined up three nails that was in a pile on my sea chest into a neat row. She studied my drawing of the chair, traced the albatross with her finger. "My father will kill me if I go back."

So she'd fought with her father—it explained the split lip and the bruise on her cheek—and now she had some romantic idea about running away to sea. "I'm sure it feels that way, miss. My own father gets powerful angry with me from time to time. But—"

"My father will kill me." She said the words louder this time. "He nearly did so last night. I have nowhere to go, Mister . . ."

"Broen," I said. "Abraham Broen."

"Mister Broen." She stood full up, which about brought her to my nose. "Forgive me. I know I take a great liberty when I ask you for a favor that puts your career and well-being at risk. I assure you I would not ask had I any other choice. Had I even one small alternative. But my mother is long dead and I have no particular friends. And it seems that, although I'd not intended to be, I am discovered. So I ask you now for your discretion. Please. Let my presence on this ship be a private matter between just ourselves. And also—" a tear spilled over. She swiped it off. "If I may prevail upon you even further, would you be so kind as to direct me to some dark, unused corner of the ship where I may hide myself for at least a portion, if not the duration, of our journey?"

Zounds. A rich Dutch girl just confessed to me that she was alone in the world and wanted to stow away on the *Lion* because she was afeared for her life otherwise.

How could a girl like her be alone in the world?

Mother dead, no friends, and a father that tried to kill her.

Or so she said.

"Prove it," I said.

"What?"

"You want me to put my head in the noose for you? Prove you're as bad off as you say you are."

"I can't think of how I can possibly do that," she said.

I waited.

The girl picked up the nails. Put 'em down again. Then held out her hands. They was cracked and red, a housemaid's hands.

"If my mother were alive, would my hands look like this?"

"Maybe."

"They wouldn't. But why would you take my word for it?" She reached for her necklace. "I can compensate you for your efforts."

I held up my hand to stop her. I didn't want her jewelry.

"What can I do to make you believe me?" she asked.

"You tell me one true thing about being alone in the world. Do that, and maybe I'll believe you."

The girl shut her mouth. Then she stuck out her chin. "Sometimes I dream I'm a canal rat. And when I wake in the morning, I wish it were true."

"Why d'you wish a thing like that?"

She gave me a half smile. "Have you never seen a canal rat, Mister Broen? They're slippery beasts, able to squeeze in and out of the tightest holes. Even the best ratters have trouble catching them. They're fat too, and not just from garbage in the canals. They eat from the best pantries in Amsterdam. And I'll tell you something else about canal rats. I've never seen one alone. They always travel in pairs at least. Why, I've seen as many as ten or twelve writhing together over our neighbor's table scraps."

She dreamed of being free, fed, and friended. So maybe she wasn't lying, then. Maybe, like me, this girl had nowhere else to go.

Up on deck, a few sailors stomped around, back from the alehouses. Any minute and they'd be coming down here. I weighed the fors and againsts of the situation. The againsts was heavy: fifty lashes, getting tied to the mast for days in all weathers, getting kicked off the ship at Cape Town, letting down Pa.

I couldn't think of any fors.

Except one.

"You're a girl," I said.

"I am," she said.

"You can sew?" I asked.

She gave me an eye. "I sew, I knit, I cross-stitch and crochet, and I've a fair hand at embroidery."

Which meant weaving cordage would be no trouble. Nor picking oakum.

"You strong?"

"Strong enough," she said. "I can carry a feather mattress down a flight of stairs and beat the dust out of it."

Not having ever seen a feather mattress myself, I had to take her word for it that she was strong. Strong enough to cut fifty staves at a go and still have strength left for fifty more? Pa said I had to do the work of two men. What if she was one of 'em? Or even half of one of 'em?

"There's a place I can think of where no one will find you and you won't be too uncomfortable."

"*Thank you,* Mister Broen—"

"You won't be too comfortable, either."

"That's no matter. I shall make do with any small space. I shall not allow one person to see me. I promise this shall be the last kindness I ask of you. I swear it."

Not likely. Staying hid would be near impossible. She'd have to ask a lot of kindnesses of me before we got to the Indies.

"But you'll have to do something for me too. I'm sticking my neck out for you, and fair's fair."

The girl got a cagey look. "As you say. If it's within my power, I shall do anything you wish."

"Oh, it's within your power. And it won't put you in danger, either. You see, I got a lot of duties, and I'm thinking you can help me with some of 'em. Things like making rope or cutting up pieces of wood."

"I shall be only too happy to help you," the girl said, looking easier. "After all, it's the least I can do."

"That's settled then. I'll take you to your new quarters." I filled a sack with a blanket, a candlestick, some candles, and a slop bucket. That done, I grabbed the lantern and moved past her into the crew's quarters. "Follow me, miss."

The crew was still mostly gone but for the German,

Kaspar Krause, who'd been sleeping off his drink since seven bells in the afternoon watch.

"Don't mind about him, miss. He's good and bowsy."

Sure enough, Krause didn't so much as crack an eye when we passed his hammock.

"Just a quick minute while I check the galley, miss."

The girl pressed her back against the mainmast, which went through the deck all the way to the bottom of the hold. I popped into the kitchen. 'Twas no more than a closet with a brick stove and racks of pots and cooking tools. Plus all kinds of grub, some of which I filched for the girl. "All clear, miss. Happy Jan the cook must still be ashore."

"Forgive me, I should have introduced myself at the beginning of our acquaintance," the girl said while we walked. She had a funny way of talking. Her fancy words fit her like a dress two sizes too big. "I'm Petra De Winter."

"Tell me, Miss De Winter—" I stopped. Might as well hammer out a few things now. "How do you plan on eating while you're aboard?"

Clearly, she hadn't thought that far ahead, but she did now. "I suppose I shall wait until the middle of the night when the ship is quiet and then I shall forage here in the galley or perhaps down in one of the holds. I see what you're thinking, Mister Broen. I know it's wrong to steal, but I shall compensate the captain when I find myself settled again."

"When the ship's quiet, you say?"

"I think that's best, don't you?"

Aye, except the ship wasn't ever quiet. There was always a watch on duty, usually at least half the crew. "And if you don't mind me asking, what's your final plan? Where do you plan to settle, since it's against the law for you to be in Batavia, which is where we're headed?"

"Against the law?" she sputtered.

"No Dutch ladies are allowed in the East Indies except family of VOC high-ups. Didn't you know that?"

"I did not." She stuck her chin out. "But I've a year to sort it out."

"Six months," I said. "De Ridder's fast."

"All the better."

"Your bunk's through there." I pointed to the next cabin. "It'll take me a minute to get it ready."

10

Petra

I followed Broen into a long, good-sized cabin that looked as though it hadn't been cleaned since Henry Hudson claimed New Amsterdam. The front end where Broen and I stood was an office. Against the near wall was a small desk covered with papers, pincers, and knives, with a quill floating in a pond of ink in the midst of the clutter. Bowls, basins, and nests of stained cloth covered a worktable, and clumps of hair and sawdust blanketed the floor. At the far end of the cabin were empty cots with a curtain that could be pulled closed for privacy but was open now. I'd visited medical men with Albertina in Amsterdam often enough to determine that this place of appalling filth was the barber-surgeon's office, where men came for a shave or a dose, depending on which they needed more.

A massive trunk doubled as a bookshelf against the long outside wall, which had two portholes that would let in a bit of air and some natural light during the day. Attached to the long inside wall was a door that ended just above my head, perhaps a foot from the ceiling, sealed with a padlock. Broen pulled a key from his pocket and started to work the lock.

"How do you happen to have the key?" I asked.

"I'm carpenter's mate. I built the storeroom," he answered without turning around. "We're lucky to have a proper surgeon. Most ships get by with the cook taking care of the doctoring—the cutting and dosing and such. But De Ridder likes to sail with a medical man. He likes it so much he had Pa and me build the cove his own digs." The lock clicked open. Broen slid it off and opened the door, revealing a large closet. "This way, Miss De Winter."

The storeroom was full of crates marked GIN and WEIN. There was just enough room for a small person to perch on top of the gin with her back against the wein. My heart sank. How was I to spend six months in such a space without being found?

"Mister Broen." I cleared my throat, which felt thick of a sudden. "You are very kind to find me any hiding place at all. And one so near a porthole and fresh air is more than I could have hoped for. It's only that I worry about being found out when the surgeon wants some of his libations."

"I see your meaning," he said, holding back a smile. "But Master Clockert bunks with the junior officers, and besides he don't want his *libations* very often, what with them being his private stash for selling in Batavia. Also, this isn't where you'll be bunking."

Ah.

He opened a hatch in the floor. I leaned over and peered into the hole where a peg-ladder disappeared into the dark.

"You'll be bunking here in the hold where all the ship's stores is stowed," he said. "This part right below us is a separate cabin for supplies we're carrying to East India—bricks, tobacco, cloth, those kinds of stuffs. No one should touch 'em for months unless we need to rebalance."

The hold. I knew little of ships but enough to understand that this would be the lowest, darkest place on board. Here I would live beneath the sea like a mole beneath the earth.

What had I done?

I straightened my back even as my spirits sank. "It's perfect."

Broen handed me the canvas sack and used his lantern to light a candle, which he put in a holder shaped like an upside-down L with two pointed ends. "You carry it around with you and stick the bottom or the side piece in the wall or wherever's handy," he explained. "But be careful, Miss De Winter. Nothing's more deadly than an open flame on a wood ship. The light should be enough for you to get stowed away, and I'll be back before long. Is there anything else you need?"

He'd already risked so much, I wouldn't dream of asking for more.

"I'm perfectly content. Thank you, Mister Broen."

"Bram," he said.

"Then you shall please call me Petra."

And I stepped down into the blackness.

11

Petra

I rubbed my arms against the chill. The air was still, cool, and heavy with damp. The hold was dark and always would be because there were no portholes. It reeked of bilge. Cloves and dried lavender would help, but of course I had none. I spun a slow circle, holding out the candle. The light showed a mountain range of crates and casks and caught the glassy eyes of rats scurrying into corners.

Much as I envied them, I hated rats. When I was small and I slept in a trundle next to Albertina's bed, they'd run across my blanket at night. I learned to sleep with the covers over my head, which was suffocating, even in winter. When I grew bigger and Tina and I shared a four-poster, I made her double knot the bed curtains.

Relief and fear dueled in my heart, with excitement and dread standing by as seconds. These would be my living quarters for the next six months. If I was lucky.

And yet, I could well understand the boy Bram's thinking. Dark, roomy, plenty of hidey-holes, and when I needed air or food, I could go up the hatch and use Master Clockert's crates to climb over his storeroom wall.

Cautiously, I explored my new home. My section of the hold was at the back end of the ship. Midship was where the everyday stores were kept. The ceiling was lower there, and barrels of water and salted meats took up a good portion of the space. The cargo was lashed together or packed in box-frames to keep it from shifting. A wall between my area and the main, everyday area would keep loose things from rolling too far.

These explorations took no more than a quarter hour. Idleness being my mind's worst enemy, I put together a makeshift sleeping platform out of two trunks, and a table from a barrel of grain. A crate of knives worked as a chair, and I used my sleeve for a duster. I lacked only a proper scrub brush and some damp sand.

When I emptied the sack, I found the supper Bram had packed for me. My fingertips began to tremble—

I tore into the stale bread. Bram had pilfered cheese too, and a stone bottle of beer, which I gulped down in one long swig. Albertina would have been appalled.

My meal finished, the pail stowed, the blanket spread, there was nothing more for me to do but sleep, and so I lay down on my new bed and wrapped myself in the blanket, which, it turned out, was very dirty but very warm.

But sleep was impossible. My mind bolted from thought to thought like a kitchen mouse with a cat after it. How would I fill the empty hours? How would I bear the loneliness? What would become of me? And, worst of all, *what had Father done to Albertina after he failed to spend all his wrath on me?* He might have beaten her or dismissed her from her position. A good job wasn't easy to find, especially without a reference from her employer. Albertina had put her own life at risk when she saved mine.

The ship rocked slowly at its mooring. I could hear the slap of the water against its hull and the creaking of its ribs. I missed the weight of nasty old Henry Hudson the cat on my feet. I pulled off my slippers and set them upside down on the end of my bed as Albertina did with hers. To ward off witches, she said.

For better or worse, tomorrow I'd be at sea.

⌇

I woke some hours later to the sound of bells. The candle had burned out and not a speck of light leaked through the ship's tightly caulked timbers. It could have been midnight or noon for all I knew. I stared into absolute darkness and wondered when Bram would return and hoped it would be soon. Then I remembered I'd sworn never to bother him again.

I'd nothing to eat. For the first time in my life, I'd nothing to do—even as a small child I'd helped my mother and Tina with the housework. I lay on my trunk bed and listened to rats skipping among the loads of cargo and sailors clomping on the floors above my head. Also a strange sweeping sound I couldn't put a name to.

I sat up.

I lay back down.

"Greetings, fellow rats," I whispered into the dark. "Please allow me to introduce myself. I am Petra De Winter, and, like you, I'm a stowaway on this ship bound for the East Indies, where, not incidentally, I've recently learned I'm forbidden by law to disembark. I've no idea how to solve that problem, and so I shall put it out of my mind until I resolve my more immediate concerns. Namely that I'm so hungry I could eat one of you vermin uncooked and in a single swallow if I could only catch you. I would steal food from the galley—as I'm sure you do on a daily basis—but judging by the thunder of sailors' feet and all the shouting and singing going on, it seems that now would not be an opportune moment."

I covered my face with my hands. "God's teeth, I'm talking to rats."

The ship's bells followed a pattern. First one bell, then, perhaps half an hour later, two bells, then three, and so on until eight. After that, they began again with one. I didn't know what the bells signified, but counting them helped pass the time.

Alas, counting bells was no help for seasickness. My stomach was no match for the sour smell of bilge and the lurch of the ship now that we were under way. I'd been on boats countless times, of course—Amsterdam is a city built on water—but I'd never felt the roll of a one-hundred-fifty-foot-long East Indiaman at sea. My nausea slithered from the pit of my stomach up my throat to squeeze my head, octopus-like, with slimy sucking tentacles. I curled up on my trunk bed and begged my body to purge itself, but the sickness neither increased nor decreased. And so I lay, sweating and counting bells, and listening to the strange sweep and shuffle somewhere above my head.

Shortly after the second round of eight, Bram came back.

"You still here, Miss Petra?" he whispered into the dark.

"I am." I pushed myself up and willed my back to stay straight. Moaning was also out of the question.

Bram carried a lantern with him and used the candle inside to light mine. "I brought you a tinderbox for when your light goes out. Some more rations too."

"Thank you."

He set another hunk of bread and some cheese on the

table. Also a bottle of beer and more candles.

"Did you go up the hatch today?" he asked.

"I didn't dare," I said. "I heard voices in the surgeon's cabin." But I needed to go up soon to empty the slop bucket through the surgeon's porthole. The smell was nearly as bad as the bilge water.

"That's no matter," Bram said. "If you take care, you should be able to stay there as long as you like. Clockert almost never unlocks the storeroom, and Krause, his mate, don't have a key. Also, I oiled the hinges on the hatch for you last night. When things settle down a bit you should be able to get some food from the galley. You'll need to, 'cause you can't get into the bread room from here. You got to go down the hatch in the gunroom to get into it."

"Where is the bread room?"

"Why, it's right there on the other side of that wall," he said, pointing to the rear of the cabin. "The bread room's got tin over all the walls to keep out rats and bugs and such. It's where we stow stuff like bread, biscuits, flour, and cheese. And also gunpowder, which is why the only way in is through the gunroom one deck up."

"You keep gunpowder with bread?"

"Can you think of a drier place?"

I couldn't.

"I'll try going up tomorrow, then. Or, er, later today? Can you tell me, Bram, what time it is? Is it day or night? I think I've worked out the bells, but I don't know the hour."

Bram said it was afternoon and he gave me an explanation of the bells that included mentions of dogs and watches and lubbers. He must have read bewilderment on my face, because he stopped his lecture and said, "Give it a few days and you'll figure it out."

"I'll make sure I do," I promised.

"We're under way. Can you tell?"

"I thought I noticed a change in pace," I squeaked.

"We're making five knots with a good steady wind. Fair skies and Barometer Piet says his hand is feeling fine."

I hadn't the slightest idea what any of that meant, but Bram seemed happy about it, so I said, "How wonderful."

"You ready to get working?"

"Absolutely," I lied. I was ready for a mercury purge.

He eyed me shrewdly. "Seasick, are you?"

"Only a bit."

"Time will take care of it. And ginger. I'll see if I can get some from Happy Jan the cook. He's got a big root of it in the galley for all the newbies who never been to sea before. Not that we have a lot of 'em, since De Ridder's got his sailors who follow him from ship to ship. I can't say about the soldiers, though. We got about a hundred on board this trip, out of maybe three hundred men total, and usually most of 'em is new to the sea."

There it was again. *Sweep, shuffle-shuffle-shuffle-shuffle.* "What's that noise?"

"Noise?"

"That sweeping, shuffling sound. I've been hearing it all day." *Sweep, shuffle-shuffle-shuffle-shuffle.*

Bram cocked his head and listened for a moment. "Only it's the soldiers moving around their quarters. They're right over your head if you're in the main part of the hold. They got their own deck there where they stay most of the time, 'cept maybe once or twice a day when they come up for air."

"Is that why the ceiling is lower in the main hold? To make a place for the soldiers?"

"Aye."

"But their deck can't be more than four feet high! A grown person can't even stand there!" Which must be why they shuffle around on their knees.

"Why, no, they can't. But that's no matter. What do they need to stand for? The soldiers don't do any ship's work—not unless we get into a battle, in which case they come out and help fight, whatever good that does, since most of 'em is next to useless. No, unless there's a battle, they mostly sleep and play cards all day."

"But why don't they work?"

"They're soldiers, not sailors, here as passengers to Batavia, where they got jobs waiting for 'em guarding the colony."

"Still, it must be uncomfortable, a hundred men sharing such a small space for six months with no room to stand. No wonder they're a rough lot. Their lives at home must be unthinkable if they were willing to sign up for this journey."

Bram's face darkened. "Sure it's uncomfortable, but when they get to the Indies they give the VOC three years labor and after that they're free to stay or go as they please. Don't seem so bad to me. 'Specially when you think about where most of 'em comes from, which is prison or the almshouse."

Something I'd said had offended Bram. I changed the subject. "Have you been on many voyages?"

"Not so many," Bram said, looking easier. "This is my second west-east crossing. The first was after my ma died and my pa came back to Batavia to get me. He's sailed with De Ridder ten years, first five as carpenter's mate and the last five as ship's carpenter. Took us nine months to sail from Java to Amsterdam 'cause we met some heavy weather and had to stop at the Cape overlong to refit. Then we hit the doldrums and we was becalmed for nearly two weeks, men dying of scurvy and fever right and left. That's when we lost our surgeon. Clockert's new. I hope he's got a better hand than Daneelszoon. That cove was slow with his knife, which is about the worst thing you can say about a ship's surgeon."

"Do you mean he was a coward? Afraid to fight?"

"I mean it took him more than twenty minutes to get a leg off when what you want is ten. Or five. The *Rijnenburg*'s got a surgeon who can do it in five."

The octopus didn't like the thought of slow amputation. I threw up into the slop bucket.

"I'll go and get that ginger," Bram said.

⁓

Hours later I was awakened by rough voices in the main part of the hold. I shot up from my bed and leaped behind a stack of crates. The octopus in my belly was gone, chased out by a woodpecker in my chest.

"Point of four."

"Making?"

"Thirty."

"Curse you, brother, for the bilking black devil you are."

"And you too, you thon of a dog."

It sounded like some men had sought out the privacy of the hold to gamble at piquet. I crept silently around boxes and barrels. A knothole in the wall between the cabins gave me a good view of them. Twins. Tall, scrawny, carbuncle-faced, no more than twenty years old. One was missing his front teeth, which explained the lisp. A barrel and two crates served as their card table and chairs, and they sat with muskets across their laps. Against the wall behind them, stacked floor-to-ceiling, were the treasure chests of the Dutch East India Company.

"You hear something?"

"Don't thtart your trickth, brother. Pay up!"

"No, I thought . . ."

He stood, a hound that had caught wind of a fox, and approached the wall I was hiding behind, the long narrow barrel of his musket pointed in front of him.

Like a poker.

The wind left my body. I was back in the front room, Father towering over me with the glowing fire iron. I could smell the olipodrigo and hear Tina shouting, *Go! Go!*

Down in the hold, I staggered through the blackness, blindly feeling my way, until I reached the hatch to the sick bay. Without stopping to listen for voices, I shoved open the trapdoor.

I clapped my hand over my mouth and squeezed my eyes against tears. I could never go home. Father would kill me if I did. Perhaps not right away, but someday after he'd had more bad news and one drink too many.

But if I never went home, I'd never see Albertina again.

"If you're here merely to adorn my doorway, you're doing a poor job of it," said a man's voice on the other side of the wall.

"Master?" said a small high voice barely louder than a whisper.

"Are you here for a medical problem?"

"Just . . . just *this*, sir."

I crawled the rest of the way out of the hatch and pressed my eye to a crack between two boards. Clockert, if the sallow-faced man with stringy brown hair drooping over half his face was indeed Clockert, sat at his desk with his jacket off and his shirtsleeves rolled up, a quill in his hand. In the doorway stood a little boy with stooped bony shoulders, and hair, skin, and eyes the color of wheat. He'd unwrapped a bloody rag to show the surgeon his forearm, which had a flap of skin the size of a florin coin dangling from it. Blood flowed to the floor in a steady trickle.

"Hmph." Clockert lifted the arm and held it up to the light. "Chisel? Splinter? Broken glass?"

"Goat, sir," the boy whispered.

"A *goat?*"

"She didn't mean to do it, sir. The goose, 'e bit the goat, and the goat, she bit me. I take care of the animals, sir. It is my job. And also I am the drummer. I 'ave two jobs, sir."

"Stop there, young man. I am quite sure I have no wish to know more about the ship's livestock. What's your name?"

"Louis Cheval, sir."

"You're a Walloon?"

"No, sir! I am French."

"And how old are you?"

"Nine." The boy's face had blanched from dry wheat to skimmed milk, but the surgeon seemed not to notice.

"How did a French boy of nine end up on a Dutch ship?"

"My parents, they are dead, sir. I went to live with my uncle, who is Dutch. 'E sent me 'ere. May I . . . if you please?"

"Ah, yes, sit down." Clockert stood and offered Louis

his chair. The boy collapsed onto the seat and dropped his tassel-topped knit cap on the floor.

"Krause," Clockert called over his shoulder, "I'm going to sew up this boy's arm. Prepare the ointment, please." Clockert opened a drawer in his desk and rummaged through various bits of stuff until he found a needle and thread.

"Krause!"

A grunt, followed by shuffling footsteps. "Sorry, master." A large, slovenly, red-nosed fellow, more boy than man, rubbed sleep from his eyes. If I wasn't mistaken, he was the drunk sailor Bram and I had seen sleeping in the crew's quarters.

"The ointment, if it's not too much trouble, my bovine colleague."

"Yes, sir."

Krause knelt beside the medical chest and began taking off stacks of books.

Clockert picked up Louis's arm and used a rag to wipe away the blood. "You're not squeamish, are you?" he asked the boy.

"Squeamish, sir?"

"You're not going to faint or vomit or scream *comme une petite fille*?"

"No, sir. I don't *think* so. At least I 'ope not."

"Krause, give the boy some gin."

"Right away, sir." The surgeon's assistant poured gin

into a cup and, when Clockert wasn't looking, took a long pull from the bottle himself.

Clockert took the cup and gave it to Louis to drink, which he did with gusto.

Brave Louis kneaded his jacket with his good hand but otherwise kept quiet while Clockert worked. I counted the stitches—nine. If I'd been wielding the needle I'd have done twelve and not tugged nearly so hard.

"Krause, the ointment."

"I'm sorry, master, I don't remember—"

Krause sat in front of the open chest, looking like a lost boy in a big man's body. Saws, knives, and other metal contraptions fanned the inside of the lid in a holster, while the main box held tiered trays with dozens of glass bottles and jars.

"It's the same one I showed you yesterday for the sail-maker's split knee. However, I do realize that two ingredients is a great deal to remember."

At home, Albertina and I used a tincture of—

"Myrtle and turpentine. Here, I'll do it myself."

Clockert quickly found the bottles he wanted and measured the oils drop by drop in a small bowl. He applied the mixture to Louis's arm and wrapped it snuggly with linen.

"Now, *Monsieur* Cheval, do be careful of goats and geese—and pigs and ducks for good measure—and come see me tomorrow so I can have a look and change the dressing."

"Thank you, sir." Louis sprang from his seat and hurried out of the cabin, forgetting his hat in his haste to be gone.

"I shall breakfast here this morning," Clockert said to Krause. "Bread and cheese, please. And coffee. Black."

"Right away, sir." Krause lumbered out of the cabin.

Clockert returned to his paperwork, his back to me. He wrote with an elbow on the desk and a hand threaded through his hair. I stared at Louis's hat and weighed all the likely outcomes of my reckless decision to stow away. If I was very lucky, I'd sneak off the ship in Batavia and find work with a Dutch family. Or what was far more likely: I'd be found out and my future would be determined by the captain. Was he a merciful man? A generous one? Surely he was practical, as any captain who runs a "tight ship" would be.

A stowaway girl discovered on a ship has few options; the stowaway daughter of Sacharias De Winter, merchant banker and former commissioner of the Amsterdam Bank of Exchange, has even fewer.

But a no-name stowaway boy . . .

I squatted down and snaked my arm through the space under the storeroom door, my fingers creeping along the floor toward Louis Cheval's hat. A stray lock of hair fell across my face. Tonight I'd ask Bram to help me cut it short. My hand inched closer—

"Halt, vermin! Who dares invade my office?"

12

Bram

"You sure Clockert didn't smoke you, Miss Petra?"

Petra looked a lot less green after a couple of days at sea and a belly full of ginger. We was down in the hold, and I was showing her how to pick oakum. Oakum's made from old ropes. You take an end and split the hairs apart with a marlin spike 'til it looks like a fuzzy nest, and then you can use bits of the nest to caulk the cracks and holes that all ships are full of. I figured with Petra picking her share down here, I'd double my daily ration.

"I'm perfectly certain he didn't see me," she said. "The surgeon was yelling at a rat—and no wonder it was there, given the state of the sick bay. He threw his shoe at it."

"He hit it?"

"He missed. The rat's probably somewhere down here now with the rest of his very large family."

"You'll be glad of those rats if we get stuck with no wind and food running low," I said.

"You don't mean—"

"Aye. They're not too bad so long as you cook 'em enough."

Petra gnawed off another chunk of ginger.

"Why'd you do it, anyway? Why risk getting smoked for a hat?"

"For that very reason: Because there's always a risk—no matter how careful we are—that I'll be caught. And if that happens, I think I'll be safer as a boy. I've worked it all out. I'll cut my hair and wear Louis's hat, and perhaps you could help me find a shirt and trousers, or I could sew them myself with some of these ridiculous skirts that make it all but impossible to climb over Clockert's storeroom wall—"

Petra's skirts did look fairly volumable, but her scheme was barmy.

"Think of it, Bram. With a pigtail and sailor's clothes, who'd know the difference?"

"Everyone, that's who. Trousers and tail or no, you'd never pass. Nobody'd believe it for half a minute. And once they smoked you for a girl, they'd know you had help with your cover-up. Then that'd lead straight to me and we'd both be sunk."

Petra made one of those airy noises with her nose that girls make. "You're right, of course. No female could get by on a ship for more than two bells without some *cove* such as yourself helping her. If I get found out looking like this, you're sure to go down with me. However . . . at least if I'm dressed as a boy, there's a chance the crew will believe I am one, and a chance they'll believe I stowed away on my own."

I gave Petra a good look-over. She'd have to get some dirt on her face and start leaning back in her chair instead of sitting on the edge with a poker up her shirt. But maybe if she cut off her hair . . .

"Be a boy."

"I beg your pardon?"

"You say you can pass for one. Show me how you'll do it."

"All right," she said, squaring her shoulders.

"Wrong," I said.

"What do you mean, 'wrong'? I haven't said anything yet!"

"It's not what you're saying; it's what you're doing. Which is sitting. Which is all wrong."

"Fine, then. Tell me how to do it properly."

"Boys slouch."

She slouched down so low, she almost slouched right off the crate.

"Not like you're dead. Like you're comfortable. Like this," I said, pointing at myself.

Petra fixed herself. Mostly.

"Better," I said. "Now say something."

"Hoay there! How now, mate!"

"Is that a joke?"

"No, it's not a joke! It's what I hear a hundred times a day, sailors shouting at each other like the whole world's gone deaf."

"That's because it's a cove on deck calling up to another cove on top of a mast. Try some regular parley. We're just two coves having a chat. And don't make your voice so deep. We're twelve, not twenty."

Petra eyed me for a bit. Then she set her knees apart, hawked up a hunk of phlegm, and spit it over her shoulder.

"How now, mate? That boy enough for you?"

My mouth dropped open. I shut it.

"You know, Miss Petra, you just might do."

"I'm so glad you think so, Mister Broen."

13

Bram

Helping Jaya the cooper make barrels was a good way for me to catch the captain's eye. 'Twas hard work and we did it outside in the waist, the open part of the upper deck that was amidships directly in view of De Ridder's quarterdeck.

Two weeks at sea, and we was well under way. The weather was cloudy but comfortable. A fresh breeze had come up and we was moving at a good clip.

Petra'd done a fair job of cutting wood staves for the barrels, and I had a batch over a fire, cooking in a pot of water 'til they got soft enough so Jaya could bend 'em. My job was to keep sponging 'em down, which was hot work and I had the blisters to prove it. Jaya's job was to winch 'em into the right shape and pound 'em into the iron loop at the bottom of the barrel. We used three dozen staves per barrel, and after four barrels we was running low.

"You have more staves, my brother?" Jaya asked.

Jaya was really Mulawarman Wijaya, but no Hogen-Mogen Dutchman could get his mouth around those names. He was a little cove, not much bigger than me, but strong. Like me, he was Indies-born, but not like me, he was full-blooded, which he never let me forget. He didn't do anything outright, but 'twas there in how he said "my brother." If you knew what to listen for, you'd know I was no brother of his.

Jaya didn't leave the Indies 'til he was full grown, and it showed in how he talked. After I was around him for a while, it showed in how I talked too.

"*Ya, Om,* I got more." Jaya was a good friend of Pa's, so I called him "uncle."

"How much is the number?"

"Don't know for sure. Plenty plenty."

"*Plenty plenty,* Brammetje," said Tixfor, one of the ship's boys. He was servant to Isaac Van Swalme, a gentry cull who repped the VOC in Batavia. As senior merchant, Van Swalme was the highest-up cove on board—higher even than De Ridder, whose cabin he shared. Tixfor thought some of Van Swalme's clout rubbed off on him. He was probably right. "Oh, yaaaa, you do every*ting* plenty plenty now. Plenty plenty staves, plenty plenty oakum, plenty

plenty paint, plenty plenty sharp sharp, plenty plenty cut cut!"

"You funny, boy," Jaya said. 'Twas a warning to Tixfor, but not much of one.

"How you do so much plenty plenty, Brammetje?" Tixfor went on, ignoring Jaya. "The men say you're a demon, you stay up all night, no sleep sleep. Is *dat* true?"

What was true was I wanted to punch him in his smart face plenty plenty.

"I think I hear your master calling you, Tix," I said.

Tixfor laughed and skipped off. Jaya spit betel nut juice into a cup he always kept with him. The stuff turned his teeth red as blood. It reminded me of my granny. She chewed betel too.

"Go and get some more staves, then," he said to me.

The staves was in the hold with Petra, so I headed aft. A blockhead mistake—in my mind I was still beating on Tixfor—'cause the room under the fo'c'sle was the other way, and that's where Jaya would expect the staves was.

"Bram," Jaya called. "Where you going?"

"To get the staves, *Om*. I stowed 'em in the hold."

"The hold? Why do you—"

"Be right back!" I called, hoping he'd let it drop if I got away fast enough.

I found Petra knee-deep in guns. She had muskets and pistols piled up around her, and a bunch of open crates told me where she'd got 'em. There was black dirt all over her face and even in her hair, which I still hadn't gotten used to, tied back in a short pigtail under her knit cap. At least her togs looked like everybody else's now. Grimy.

"What are you *doing*?" I whispered.

"Cleaning guns," she said. "I've gone through all the rope you left me, and the rest of the staves are over there." She pointed to a neat bundle leaning against the bulkhead.

The guns was brand-new, but I couldn't stop to wonder why Petra thought they needed cleaning. She was no lazy rich girl, I'd give her that. She did all the work I brought her and asked for more. She wanted to know the names of all the ship's parts and the crew, so I drew 'em in my sketchbook for her and she flipped through the pages over and over until she had it all fixed in her head. Petra didn't know why I wanted her to do my work. No reason to go into all the ins and outs of being a no-name by-blow. So she didn't savvy why it did me no good for her to clean up a bunch of guns with no one the wiser. And with Jaya maybe coming after me, I had no time to explain it to her.

"I'm sure the guns look much better now, Miss Petra, but even so, you got to pack 'em all up."

"But I haven't finished yet!"

"I know, but—"

"You are here, Bram?"

Jaya.

"Hide, Miss Petra," I whispered. "Quick!"

She was up before I got the words out, and away into the dark.

"Bram?" Jaya called again.

I kicked Petra's slippers into a corner, then grabbed the staves and ran out to the main hold.

"Bram, what are you—"

"Sorry, I was just getting these," I said, holding up the staves.

Jaya sized me up good. I stared back 'til my eyes hurt from looking innocent.

"You are hiding something." He spit into his cup. "I know this."

Sweat ran down the side of my face. I could smell my own fear, and I bet Jaya could smell it too.

"What you hide, Bram?"

I didn't give him an answer, so Jaya started looking. He moved slow, going from box to box, from tarp to tarp.

Petra could be behind any one of 'em.

"You got it wrong, *Om*," I said. "There's nothing going on. *Ayo*, please, let's go finish the barrels."

"We finish barrels after I find what you are hiding."

Jaya pushed past me and went into Petra's back room, where he found four boxes of the VOC's best new guns spread over the floor.

"I thought it was funny you keep staves in hold and not in cabin where you make them," Jaya said, shaking his head. "That is why I come down here. Maybe you have some food, bottle of gin, maybe some tobacco. But no. You have guns. Why you do this, my brother? You think you sell guns when we are in Batavia? You think you make big big money that way? VOC pay is so small that you— and me—we are like coolies. Slaves. Is that why you do this?"

What was worse? Slipping Petra or letting Jaya think I was a thief? Men got hanged for a lot less than filching guns. If I said nothing, I'd swing for sure. But if I slipped Petra, Jaya would think she was the thief and she'd swing for me.

Before I could answer him, Jaya raised his arm and I set my teeth against the blow. But the slap landed on my back, not my face.

"I understand, my brother."

"You do?"

"*Ya*. But this is not the way. You are too small and too lonely to steal guns. Put them back now."

Before Jaya could change his mind, I scooped up an armful of muskets and loaded 'em into a crate.

"You are quick boy. Very smart. Very hard work," Jaya said, watching me. "You should have money. But this is not the way, my brother."

My brother. 'Twas the first time he'd said the words like he meant 'em.

14

Bram

"Miss Petra, I brought you a treat!"

After a month at sea, everyone'd eaten most of what they brought with 'em, and treats was rarer than a blue moon. I came down the ladder and stuck my candlestick in the wall. Petra was standing stock-stiff next to her bed, looking like I'd caught her at something.

"A treat?" she said.

"Aye, look and see."

I handed her a small jar. Petra pried off the top and looked inside.

"Is it—?"

"Aye. Honey. A cove gave it to Pa after he fixed his sea

trunk for him, and Pa gave some to me. Here's a biscuit to go with it."

But Petra didn't take the biscuit. She just stood there with her nose in the jar.

"Miss Petra?"

"Hmm? Oh! Forgive me. Th-thank you, Bram. Thank you very much for sharing your treat with me."

Petra looked odd. Her eyes was all puffy like she'd been crying, and her hands shook a little.

"The honey's meant for eating, not for sniffing," I said, trying a joke.

She might've gone red. I couldn't tell in the dim light.

"Yes, I know. It's just that the honey smells so good, and, well . . ."

I knew what she meant. The honey smelled like honey, and the hold stank of dirty water and dead rats.

We ate ship's biscuits and honey and talked for a bit, and Petra's hands stopped shaking and her face started looking more regular.

"Did you bring more oakum for me?" she asked.

"Not today. You picked all a cove could possibly do twice over yesterday. It'd seem off if I showed up with more."

Her face was grim, like she was sorry she didn't have more neck-cracking, finger-pricking work to do. It must be dull as doors down here. I looked round her quarters.

The boxes was stacked so each one lined up just so with the next. And they was grouped in size order with—I counted—exactly six boxes in every stack. The barrels was grouped in fours—four together on the bottom, four on top—lined up like the boxes so no edge hung over another. I bet if I wiped the floor, my hand would come away clean.

This was what Petra did when there was nothing else to do. And when she ran out of stuff to straighten, I bet she did it all over again.

"Pretty dull down here?" I asked.

"Oh, I make do," she said, her hands shaking again. "There are always rats to chase, and I make up stories for myself . . . poems . . . that sort of thing. It's quite nice, actually, no one telling me what to do. I can sleep as much as I want! I've grown quite lazy."

Sweep, shuffle-shuffle-shuffle.

"And then, of course, there are the soldiers, right up there, just a few feet from my head. So it's not as if I'm alone. Not really."

She said all this cheerly enough, but she said it too fast and too bright.

"What's that?" I asked, pointing at a pile of rags on her perfectly neat bed.

"This?" she said, holding up the pile. "It's nothing. Just a doll I made for company. Twelve is too old for dolls, but I just thought . . . under the circumstances . . ."

The thing was made of linen scraps with charcoal eyes and oakum hair. 'Twas the saddest, ugliest doll I'd ever seen.

Rats, dolls, and soldiers. I'd brought Petra down here. Now I had to get her out.

15

Petra

One month underwater. One month in the dark. One month in the bilge.

But also one month with no new bruises, no swellings, no loose teeth.

In those long hours I'd learned many things. I'd learned that ships leak, no matter how much oakum plugged their cracks. I'd learned that splinters from rope were impossible to pluck out, no matter how fine the needle. I knew what time the bells signified and the difference between the first dog watch and the last dog watch. From Bram's sketches I knew all the ship's parts and some of the men. I knew how to tie a becket hitch and how to flemish a line, and I could mend a torn sail well enough to earn Bram the nickname "sew sew boy."

I'd grown used to the hard, salty food. I'd even grown used to the rats; they were much smaller than Father, after all.

But I missed air.

By day I worked at whatever task Bram brought down for me, and by night I crawled up through the surgeon's quarters to the galley to steal food. Portholes were kept closed while the ship was under way, even in calm weather. When there was no one sleeping in the sick bay I stuck my face up to a grate and breathed.

Which was why, when Bram came in the middle watch and offered to take me outside, tears sprang to my eyes, and my hands shook so I could hardly straighten my shirt laces.

Bram had lookout duty. With little wind and no need to change course, only the officer on watch would be awake on deck navigating the ship with the helmsman out of view in the steering house. Bram assured me that so late at night, the rest of the crew on duty—some sixty-five men—would be asleep at their posts. When he climbed the mast to his post in the crow's nest, I'd go with him.

"There's a new moon and no stars tonight. No one'll notice you in the dark. Or if they do, they'll think you're Louis. We should be safe enough so long as we're quiet," Bram said.

"I won't make a sound," I swore.

"It's just like climbing a tree," he said. "And when you get to the top, there's nothing but sky and air for miles."

Sky and air for miles!

We passed through the orlop deck, which was directly above the hold. Except for my visits to the barber-surgeon's office and the cook's galley, I hadn't been on the orlop since the night I met Bram. We made our way through the long crew cabin, threading among sailors in hammocks strung with hardly an inch between them. Even on a night like tonight, with all the grates open, the air was sour soup. I could only imagine what it was like for the soldiers, trapped half a deck lower with no grates at all.

From the orlop, we climbed through a hatch to the waist, the middle portion of the upper deck that was open to the sky. The sleeping crew on watch there were wedged between cannons called big guns. No one stirred as we snaked among them, little more than shadows, to the forecastle deck, at the front, or "bow," of the ship. The fo'c'sle was where the crew worked and took leisure. From Bram's drawings I knew that its mirror at the back, or "stern," was the quarterdeck, a place where only officers and important passengers were allowed to go.

I took in great heaving lungfuls of sea air.

"What are you doing?" Bram whispered.

"Breathing," I said.

"Well, do it quieter."

A fine mist hung in the air and clung to every rope and

rail. The only sounds were the creaking of the hull and the occasional flop of a loose sail in the light wind.

Bram pointed aft where Majoor stood at the rail on the quarterdeck, dimly lit by a horn lantern. Bram had explained to me that as officer on watch, it was Majoor's job to oversee the steering of the ship. If the *Lion* needed to change course—unlikely in this calm—Majoor would wake the men on watch so they could adjust the sails and he'd call the order to the helmsman in the steering house. One of the oddest things I'd learned about ships was that the person doing the steering did it from a narrow cabin with no view of the sea. The officer on watch would tell him to head east or west or north or south a few degrees and he'd move the whipstaff accordingly, the whipstaff being a pole as tall as a man that shifted the ship's tiller that in turn moved the ship's keel—a piece of wood shaped like a fin that was attached to the ship's bottom, which, when moved, shifted the ship's course.

It was all very odd indeed.

I crouched down behind a pile of rope.

"Hoay, Mister Majoor!" Bram called.

"That you, Broen?"

"Aye, sir."

"O'Brian'll be glad to see you."

There was a thud, followed by a shadow rising from the deck at the foot of the mainmast. O'Brian had come down from his post.

"Think I'll look out from the foremast tonight, Mister Majoor," Bram said. "*Bene darkmans,* O'Brian."

"*Bene darkmans,*" O'Brian said, yawning. He handed Bram the spyglass before shuffling off.

Bram stowed the glass in his belt and whispered into my ear, "Hop onto the rail, take hold of the rigging, and climb it like a ladder."

The rail was a wood fence around the edge of the ship that kept people from falling overboard. Climbing onto it was easy enough. There were plenty of ropes—*lines,* I corrected myself—that I could hold on to.

Swaying gently with the motion of the *Lion,* I studied the rigging, a grid of rope that stretched from the rail to the top of the mast. At least I assumed it went to the top, since the mast disappeared in the mist far above our heads. I reached out and tugged on the rigging. It moved.

I glanced down at Bram, who gave me a thumbs-up. Whatever Bram claimed, climbing the rigging would not be like climbing a tree, since trees didn't tend to do things like bounce.

Bram gave me a little push. "Go on," he mouthed.

I put one foot onto the rigging and felt it sink. But I imagined the view from the clouds and willed myself to keep going. First one hand, then the other. And now the second foot.

The rigging swung in toward the mast, and I squeezed my eyes shut, praying my nose wouldn't break with the impact.

To my relief, I stopped well short. I let out my breath and began to climb, one hand, then one foot at a time.

After a few minutes, I felt Bram grab on below me. It was slow going. I'd no trust in the lines; they moved too much. Unused to this heavy work, I grew tired.

I looked down, past Bram to the deck. He'd told me that the masts were close to a hundred feet tall. I'd traveled perhaps ten.

One hand, one foot. One hand, one foot. Every muscle wound tight as a corset string. My arms began to shake and then my legs too. I looked down again. Twenty feet now, eighty more to go. Bram hung easily, waiting for me to take another step. I stopped.

"What's the matter?" Bram whispered.

"I—I'm not strong enough. I don't think I can do it."

"Little Louis climbs all day. If he can, you can," Bram said.

I burned with shame. Freedom was some eighty feet up, but I couldn't get there because I was weaker than a nine-year-old boy.

"I'm coming down," I whispered.

"But Miss P—"

I ignored Bram's quiet protests and climbed down as fast as I could. He'd no choice but to let me.

Once we reached the deck, I fled through the orlop and down to the hold. Down, down, down. Away from air and mist and sea.

"What happened up there?" he said. "It's no worse than a tree."

"I wouldn't know. I've never climbed a tree," I told him.

"Never? Never once?"

I held my tongue, and he looked at me with scorn, or perhaps pity, which only magnified my shame.

"We'll go again another night, Miss Petra."

I shook my head.

"As you wish," he said. "But don't think of trying again unless I'm with you. It's too dicey."

As if I would try again. As if I *could* try again.

"Promise you won't go up without me."

It was an easy promise to make.

16

Petra

In a battle between hunger and humiliation, hunger wins. After my failure at the mast, I wanted nothing more than to curl up with the rats in their nests—which they rebuilt no matter how many times I swept them away—until I shriveled into some unidentifiable piece of cargo, too wooden for food, too fleshly to be of use.

It took about ten hours for my stomach to reject that plan. Ten hours until the ship's biscuit in my pocket threatened to bore a hole straight into my empty stomach and the salt beef I'd stowed in a gun crate called my name.

With a full belly came humility. And resolve. I was weak. I could grow stronger.

In the morning when the crew was working at their loudest, I shifted cargo and hung thick lines from the beams in the ceiling until I had a gymnasium like the Greeks used to train their athletes. Well, perhaps not so like the Greeks', but good enough to train a puny girl to climb a mast. The next morning, and every morning thereafter, while the crew banged the deck clean with holystones, I climbed and jumped and swung, picturing the look on Bram's face when I told him I'd never climbed a tree. He thought me a wealthy girl of leisure. Wealthy, I might once have been; leisured, I never was; strong enough to climb the mast, I'd be.

Having a goal gave purpose to my days, and I relished my sore muscles. I cried less and my hands stopped shaking.

At night I left my lair to forage. After four weeks, I scarcely gave my trousers and short pigtail a second thought, except to marvel at the freedom they gave me each time I climbed a ladder without tripping over my skirts or ran a comb over my head in seconds instead of minutes. In spare moments, of which I had countless down in the hold, I counted the ways in which it is preferable to be of the female sex. The list stood at zero.

About a fortnight after I built my gym, I crept into the sick bay to check my patients. I called them mine, though they knew me only through fevered dreams. A young sailor slept deeply, his broken leg splinted and propped on a sack of sawdust. I pressed the inside of my wrist against his forehead—cool—and moved to the next bed.

Diederick Van Assendorp sweated in a fitful sleep after

a day of flux. The commander of the soldiers was a big man with a wide scar that ran from his ear to the corner of his mouth and gave him a fierce look even at rest. I held his head and gave him a little barley water. He never opened his eyes.

Caring for the sick, doing whatever odd jobs Bram had for me, these were my attempts to earn my passage. But my patients didn't know I cared for them, and only Bram knew about the work I did. Should I be caught, I'd have only my maleness for protection.

Perhaps there was more I could do, work that was mine alone that would prove my usefulness and earn me goodwill. I looked around the filthy sick bay. My candle gave enough light to see dirty rags, scalpels, piles of hair and other bits. The room needed a thorough fumigation.

It was a place to start.

And from there? The orlop was packed with sleeping men; I could spend no time in those quarters. But outside was another matter. Bram and I had proved I could move about without being noticed if the weather was right. There were plenty of lines to straighten, sails to patch, metal to polish.

Also, plenty of air.

I'd promised Bram I wouldn't try to climb the mast without him, and I'd keep that promise. But surely he wouldn't mind too much if I made myself useful, so long as I was careful.

And if he never knew, how could he mind at all?

I snuffed my candle, then tiptoed through the crew's quarters and crawled under men sleeping shoulder to shoulder in their hammocks. The smell there was thick enough to stick to the back of a spoon. I hurried up to the waist.

The night was cool and clear. I glanced toward the bow at the fo'c'sle deck. Full of men, all sleeping. Behind me on the quarterdeck, First Mate Van Plaes stood watch in shadows, his boney face aglow by lantern light. I could make out his sunken eyes and hollow cheeks, but he couldn't see me, hidden behind a sail. I tilted my head back, squinting up the mast where I knew the crow's nest would be, though it was too dark to see the small platform. One night after I grew strong enough, I'd climb the rigging like a proper sailor and gaze all the way to the horizon.

I kept my eye on Van Plaes as I crept from shadow to shadow, coiling a tangled line, adjusting the tarpaulin cover on a cannon. When I reached the bow, I took a bundle from inside my jacket—what was left of my girl clothes. I'd used some of the material to make my trousers and shirt. Now I took the rest and cast it into the sea. I felt nothing but relief. These clothes were the last things that connected me to my former life.

Well, nearly the last. I unclasped the gold cross my father had given me when I took my First Communion at five. He'd had it inscribed with his name, as though to remind me that his power in my life was second only to God's. The Dutch Reformed Church was my father's religion, my mother having left the Church of England to marry him. I had no special affection for the necklace and none at all for my father. I drew back my arm, ready to cast the thing into the sea, but then I thought that the necklace was the only thing of value I owned. If I ever reached Batavia, I might be glad to have it for barter. I put it on again, tucked out of sight inside my shirt.

Back down to the galley. Happy Jan's kitchen would have impressed even Albertina. A fine layer of sawdust coated the floor, ready for whatever dripped on it in the morning. Knives, spoons, and bowls were clean and neatly stowed. An oiled pot gleamed in the hearth over a banked fire, and the brick oven was swept of ash. There were rations here for three hundred men. Surely no one, not even the meticulous Happy Jan, would notice what I'd taken. *Stolen*, I reminded myself. I loaded my pockets with food for the morrow—ship's biscuits, hard as lead but filling, and salt pork.

A bowl of speckled eggs sat on a shelf, ready to be coddled for the captain's breakfast. Fresh food! Food that hadn't been preserved in salt or hardened with time. My mouth watered at the thought of an egg sliding cool and raw down my throat. There were nine in the bowl. Would Happy Jan miss one?

I reached out a hand—

"What you doing in my kitchen?"

I'd never seen Happy Jan, but I'd had a picture of him in my mind based on his name and immaculate kitchen. He'd be plump and rosy cheeked, with a fringe of white hair and a heavy limp from an old battle wound. His jacket buttons would shine and his breeches, newly tarred and waterproof, would freshen the kitchen with the scent of pine.

Except Happy Jan was as tall as Father and even broader. His forearms, which I could see because he wore no jacket and his shirtsleeves were rolled, were corded with muscle. In the glow of his lantern, his dark skin shone like eggplant, the whites of his eyes gleamed like butter. Columns of small scars carved ladders in his cheeks.

Happy Jan looked anything but happy.

But I reminded myself that my looks also belied my name. With a pigtail, short baggy trousers, and loose shirt, I looked like a ship's boy. Like Louis Cheval's blonder brother. Why shouldn't he believe the ruse? I widened my stance and slouched, just as Bram had taught me.

"Beg your pardon, Mister Happy Jan, sir," I said. "I'm here for my master."

Happy Jan narrowed his yellow eyes at me. "Your master?"

My brain scrolled through the roster of men I'd seen in Clockert's cabin during my spying sessions.

"*Seigneur* Van Swalme, sir." Isaack Van Swalme came to Clockert to trim his remarkable beard every Tuesday and Friday, and his authority on the *Golden Lion* was greater even than the captain's. So long as Happy Jan didn't already know Tixfor, Van Swalme's manservant, I should be safe.

"Where's Tixfor?"

Luck had turned her back on me. But I'd an excuse ready.

"Tix is in the sick bay, sir. He's got flux."

"Flux," Happy Jan repeated.

"Yes, sir." I held my breath.

"Why you come in here, then?"

"For . . . for an egg, sir. *Seigneur* Van Swalme is having trouble sleeping and he was hungry."

The extravagance of eating eggs in bed in the middle of the night clearly offended Happy Jan. "These are the captain's eggs."

"Aye, sir. *Seigneur* Van Swalme hoped the captain could spare—I mean, my master wanted to know if the captain could maybe give him one."

I had to mind my tongue. My educated speech could give me away as easily as my straight back.

Happy Jan stared down at me, and I prayed the light was too dim in the galley for him to see the bulges in my pockets. Then he held his hand over the bowl, skimming each egg in turn, making his selection. At last he extracted the smallest, careful not to jostle the others, and held it out on his calloused palm.

"Thank you, sir." I stopped myself from curtsying just in time. "Compliments from *Seigneur* Van Swalme."

Happy Jan curled back his lips, revealing teeth that were filed into sharp points like rows of daggers. Any piece of flesh that passed between those lips would come out bloody—if it came out at all. He leaned toward me until my nose was but an inch from his mouth.

"Go."

I needed no second invitation. I fled the galley to the hold, and my heart didn't slow until I collapsed onto a crate.

I'd done it! Happy Jan might have thought me a thief, but he'd thought me a boy thief!

I rolled the egg between my palms. The shell was warm. I gave it a sharp one-handed crack against the edge of the crate, threw back my head, and swallowed.

17

Bram

"Hey, Bram, how'd you sleep last night?" Tixfor asked.

The weather was foul and I was cleaning paintbrushes in the carpenter's cabin. From the smug look on his pretty-boy face, Tixfor'd stopped by to torture me.

"I slept fine, thanks."

"That so? Slept all night here with your pa? Never even got up for a piss?"

"Why're you so concerned with how and when I piss, Tix?"

"No reason. It's just that five lines were freshly whipped this morning with a wrap stitch the bosun didn't know, and the sailmaker woke up with his royal cobbled. Now everyone's wondering who did it." Tixfor cleaned under his nails with the corner of a chisel. My chisel. "Some are saying it was you. Nobody can figure how you've been doing the work of two men, especially when your pa says you've been sleeping next to him all night. It's a rare cove who can be in two places at once, if you ask me."

"I wasn't asking." I straightened up. "And it wasn't me who whipped the lines or fixed the royal." But I knew who it had to be.

"Wasn't anybody else, either. Half the men think we've got a selkie woman aboard who's shed her skin, and the other half think we've got a sea devil and maybe he's you."

"What do you think?"

"Whoever it is has got a way with a needle. I say he's a sew sew boy with a sense of humor."

Sew sew boy was the name Petra'd earned me with her rows of tight stitches no man aboard could match.

The punishment for fighting was flogging. If it was anything less—

"Let me know when you find your man, Tix. Thanks for coming by."

Soon as he swagged off, I bolted for the hold.

Petra was cutting bandages out of linen for the surgeon's rag box. I swiped the whole lot onto the floor. "What do you think you're doing!"

Her mouth hung open like a hooked fish before she answered. "Er, what you asked me to do. Making bandages."

She picked up a handful and brushed at 'em. "They're dirty now."

"That's not what I meant." It hurt my throat not to yell. "I meant last night. When you went up on deck after you promised you wouldn't."

"I didn't promise I wouldn't go up on deck—"

"You did!"

"I promised I wouldn't try to climb the mast," she said, smoothing out the linen. "And I didn't."

"But you did plenty of other things, didn't you? The lines, the royal . . ."

"I was trying to be useful! I don't understand why you're angry."

"I'm angry 'cause everyone thinks 'twas me who did it!" I said.

"But you should be glad, then," Petra said, looking up at me from her seat on a beer cask. "Aren't you always looking for more work to do?"

"I'm not glad, because the whole ship knows I was in my hammock all night with my pa. So now they figure I must be some kind of sea devil working magic in my sleep."

"Oh," Petra said. "I see. Well, that is a problem." She fingered the linen for a minute, thinking. "You'll just have to tell them it wasn't you."

"You don't know many sailors, do you? They're a superstitious lot. They won't believe me 'til they see the real devil in the flesh, which, in this case, happens to be you. So we're stuck."

'Twas starting to sink in for her, the mess she'd made. "I'm sorry," she said. "I'm trying to find ways of paying for my passage—and of proving my worth, should I be found out. And, I admit, I wanted a bit of air."

"You wanted air? If you'd wanted air, you should have stayed in Amsterdam!"

"If I'd done that," she said, her voice tight as a winched line, "I'd be dead. If I'd had anyplace else to go, I'd have gone there. I'm sorry to burden you, Bram, but you've no idea what it's like, being trapped."

Petra had that scared dog look she had the night she boarded. I knew where the look came from—she told me the night I found her in Grof's locker. All this time, I'd kept my problems to myself, and she'd done everything I asked her, no questions asked. I owed her more than that.

"I might know what it's like," I said. "Didn't you wonder why I was aboard that first night when the rest of the crew'd gone ashore?"

I told her then. About the certificate and why I needed to work so hard for De Ridder.

"If you can't go to Amsterdam, why don't you go back to Java?" she asked.

"For what? My ma's dead and my granny too. In the East Indies, mixed-race boys aren't much better off than slaves. In the West Indies, mixed-race boys *are* slaves. In the American colonies too."

Petra had nothing to say to that.

"What'll you do when we get to Batavia?" I asked her.

"I've thought it through," she said. "Now that I'm a boy, I can land there and find a ship to take me somewhere else as crew."

So she was going to live like me. Sail from port to port with no place to call home.

"And when you can't be a boy anymore?"

She'd nothing to say to that, either. We both knew what happened to girls on their own. If they got lucky, they'd find some kind of honest work, maybe in a laundry, where they'd stir pots of hot lye 'til their eyes gave out and then die poor in the almshouse. And if they didn't get lucky, they'd find worse work in a brothel and die before they had a chance to grow old. Or they'd find a cove to marry, and depending on the cove, that could be worst of all.

18

Bram

'Twas the end of our second month at sea and the weather was fine, so the crew was dancing the Pickleherring in the waist. On dry nights, the captain let everyone jig after supper. Wood shoes on a wood deck made fair drums, and Piet Pietersen was more than a fair pipe player.

Lobo the gunner was spinning like a top in the middle of the crowd, gold earrings catching the lantern light. That cove may have been Portuguese, but he could jump like a boglander. Me, I usually stood off to the side and clapped along. Not tonight, though. Even in the shadows, I could see the looks I got from the crew, wondering was I man or monster. Tixfor was monkeying around with a couple of other coves. When he stuck his thumbs in his ears and waved his fingers like horns, I took off for the bow, where no one would bother me.

I could just make out the lion keeping watch over the sea.

"Three million florins. Gold, silver, and copper."

I knew that voice even at a half whisper. Jaya. He was up on the fo'c'sle deck with a giant who could only be Kosnik the smith. Kosnik stood more than a head taller than Jaya on legs like tree trunks. I ducked under the bowsprit so they wouldn't see me.

"It should be ours, my brother. We earned it." Jaya had to be talking about the VOC payroll. "Van Swalme, the officers, even Dutch housemaids have shares of VOC. Every florin the VOC makes, they get a piece. But we are too poor to buy stock. Our little wages come only when we get to Batavia—*if* we do not die from fever or flux or get shot or fall overboard—and only after purser steals his share."

"*Tak*," said Kosnik. "We be working all day all night in rain, wind, snow, sun and eating old food not good enough for dead dog. No wife, no kids, no going home for months, years. Most of us not getting back home alive."

"And they make all the money," Jaya said.

"*Tak*," Kosnik said. "What you be wanting me to do?"

"Not much. Not at first," Jaya said. "We go slow slow now. But later, when we get near Indies, we need your help."

"What help?"

"You do what you do so well, my brother. When time comes for us to get away, you help load trunks. They heavy heavy. And when we come to Indies, you build forge. The coins and bars, they have VOC stamp on them. Like this, we cannot use them. But after you melt and make new bars . . ."

"We being rich men."

Jaya squeezed one of Kosnik's barrel arms. "You understand."

"Is good idea," said the giant. "But we be going back now. They be missing us."

They headed aft to the dancing. I leaned against the rail and stared at the lion's ears, which was winking gold on and off in the starlight.

They're aiming to steal the VOC payroll.

19

Bram

The next morning, Pa and me was in our cabin tying on our belts, getting ready for breakfast.

"Pa, I need to tell you something."

"What's that, Brammetje?"

Nothing's private on a ship with three hundred men. I waved him close so I could whisper in his ear. "There's a plan to steal the Dutch East India Company payroll."

"I know."

"You know?"

He clapped a hand over my mouth. "Shhhh! Aye. Stay out of it. You're trying to get on the captain's good side, remember?"

I knew what he was getting at. To steal the payroll, the men would have to throw over the captain, which was mutiny. I'd get hanged if I had any part in it. But what if Jaya and his mates mutinied and De Ridder couldn't write the letter? Then I was back to where I was now—a penniless no-name cove, stuck at sea.

"There's just a few coves in on it so far and they can't go it alone," Pa said. "Nothing will come of it. And even if they try, I'm no turncoat and neither are you."

No, I wasn't a cat-in-pan, and I wasn't a thief, either. But if I didn't get that letter, I was nothing.

Louis Cheval came running in, all out of breath. "Come quick, *monsieur*," he said to Pa. "The surgeon needs you!"

"What's amiss, Louis?"

"Barometer Piet Pietersen, *monsieur*. Please! Come quick!"

Pa ran through the orlop with me following after. Seemed like half the crew was outside the sick bay pushing to get in. Against the wall O'Brian was on his knees, crying and tearing at his hair. "I didn't . . . I didn't mean to do it!" Me and Pa shoved our way inside.

"You asked for me, Master Clockert?" Pa said.

The surgeon pushed his hair off his face and looked up from Barometer Piet, who was tied to the table, shaking in a pool of his own blood with an iron spike sticking out of his belly.

Zounds.

"I did," Clockert yelled so's to be heard over the hub-bub. "That drunken, slavering specimen of seamanship outside my infirmary fell from the foremast and had the good fortune of landing on Mister Pietersen. Alas, Mister Pietersen had the ill fortune of landing on this hand-spike." Clockert touched the spike with a finger and Piet howled like a banshee.

Pa's face went pale under his freckles, but he didn't flinch. "How can I help, master?"

"I'd like you to hold Mister Pietersen's legs, if you would be so kind, while I remove the object. Mister Jaya here has offered to steady his shoulders."

Jaya spit betel juice through red teeth into his cup.

Clockert lined up a store of knives, saws, and other me-dicinal contraptions. "Krause!" he called.

Krause was leaning on the wall with his eyes shut, look-ing about as stoved up as Barometer Piet. At his master's order, Krause hauled himself up and wove his way to the table. I'd lay five florins he'd been at Clockert's brandy stores again and was deep cut.

"Mister Pietersen, can you hear me?" Clockert shouted while he tied on a stained apron.

"Aye, m-master," panted Barometer Piet.

"I'm going to remove the spike. It will hurt a great deal, but you must not move, do you understand?" Piet groaned. Clockert stuffed a wood dowel in his mouth. "Bite."

Piet's mates crowded in closer to the table.

"Gentlemen! Some leeway, if you please!" ordered Clockert. "And I must have quiet."

The men shut up and shuffled back. Jaya leaned on Barometer Piet's shoulders, and Pa took hold of his ankles. Piet had a tattoo of a rooster on top of one foot, a pig on top of the other, and crosses on both soles. If he ever fell overboard, the bird and the swine would keep him from drowning; the crosses would keep away sharks.

"Be over in a minute, Piet," one of his mates called out.

"Hey, Piet, any storms coming up today?" said another.

Barometer Piet groaned again.

"Now then, Krause. After I remove the spike, you take this cloth and clear away the new blood. I warn you, there will be a lot of it. I shall want you to hold the wound open with these forceps whilst I repair the internal damage."

"Yes, sir," Krause wheezed.

With one fast yank, Clockert slid out the spike. Barometer Piet squealed like a pig around the dowel. Blood poured out of the hole and spilled down his sides. Krause dabbed at it like a fancy lady with tea in her saucer. Can't say I blamed him. I was only too glad 'twas him doing the dabbing, not me.

"Krause!" Clockert spread the hole with his pliers and held out the handles. Krause stuck out a shaky arm for 'em, swayed, and passed out.

"Get this useless drunkard off my floor!" shouted Clockert.

Two sailors dragged Krause away.

"Is there someone who can assist me without unmanning himself?"

Everybody shifted their feet and looked away. Piet would likely die if he stayed with his belly open much longer. All kinds of bad humors could get in there. He'd always been decent to me. I knew I should help him.

"A volunteer?"

More shuffling and sideways looks. Barometer Piet stuck his neck out, begging us with his eyes. I wanted to step up, but I couldn't take my own eyes off the blood on the floor.

"In that case, I shall be my own assistant."

Piet's life was leaking out of his belly, but our bellies was too yellow to do anything about it. I looked anywhere but at Pa—at Piet, turning gray on the table, at the blood—

At Petra climbing over the storeroom wall.

She crashed to the floor, and there was shouts from every which way while she pushed her way to Clockert. Paying no mind to the hubbub, he tilted the handles of the pliers at her. Without a word, Petra took 'em and stood by his side, cool as ice, holding open the hole and mopping up blood while Clockert rooted around inside Barometer Piet with a pair of long pincers.

"Mister Pietersen, I see you were making oakum," he muttered, pulling out a clump and dropping it on the floor. He dug some more. "You were very lucky with the angle of the fall. A man can live with half a rib, but not without his liver. *Unus, duo, tres,* and . . . out it comes."

Barometer Piet's eyes rolled back in his head and he fainted. Clockert held up a piece of bone and scrutinized it in the light. The men flinched. 'Cept me. I was staring at Petra. *What were you thinking?* She shrugged: *I have no idea.* I shook my head: *You ruined us.* She bit her lip: *I know.*

"I'm glad to see there is one man aboard who isn't squeamish at the sight of a little blood. I shudder to imagine our odds should we engage in combat," Clockert said to Petra while he stitched Barometer Piet's belly.

"Yes, sir," she said. And then, because she was Petra, she added, "Perhaps just one more stitch there at the end, master?"

Clockert paused with his needle in the air and looked down his nose at her. "As you wish." He added the extra stitch and tied off the end. "And now that this matter is successfully concluded, perhaps you'd care to explain what you were doing in my private storeroom?"

20

Petra

I stood outside the captain's door, flanked by the twin sailors who'd played piquet next to the VOC trunks, and wishing with all my heart that I'd been born with a working brain. A cow was more intelligent than I. A sea slug, a crab, a Dodo bird. *Cor the baker's boy who wore no mitt.* The moment I'd feared most of all came about not by chance but because of my own recklessness. All my plans, all my care was for naught.

And what would happen to Bram if the captain connected him to me?

"You know what happenth to thtowawayth?" the toothless one asked. He and his twin were a head taller than I, and I had a view straight up their noses, which were none too clean.

"Skipper tosses 'em over with a couple o' stones in their pockets. At least that's what I seen," said his brother, wiggling his nostrils with enthusiasm.

"Ith that all? They don't get a hundred flickth of the cat firstht? Nithe and thalty?"

"Don't know. Happy Jan is close with his salt. Might use galley embers instead."

Whipped with salt and fire! I swallowed the bile that came up my throat.

"Courthe, he could alwayth keelhaul him."

"Keelhaul?" The word was out of my mouth before I could swallow it. I didn't want to know more.

"You don't know about keelhauling?" The twin with teeth put an arm around my shoulders. "It's what happens to men at sea who break the law somehow. Like by stealing. Or stowing away. It's a simple thing. Someone ties a rope around the criminal who did the bad thing. Then they toss him in the water."

"Bu . . . but what if he can't swim?"

"Oh, that's no matter. He don't have to know how to swim, because the men on deck do all the work for him. The criminal gets dragged underwater, see, from one side of the ship to the other, past the keel. That's why it's called *keelhauling*."

"But won't the person drown?"

"Only if the men doing the dragging take their time about it." He gave my shoulder a friendly squeeze. "But you don't have to worry about that, mate. We'll be quick."

"No," said the toothless brother, "the thing you got to worry about ith barnacleth."

"Bar—"

"The little black shellfish that's stuck to the sides of the hull? Those shells is mighty sharp. Sharp enough to flay the skin off a man's face. I've even seen a man lose an arm."

"I've theen one looth hith head."

"Captain will see you now."

An elderly bewhiskered man poked his head around the door. A bluish white film covered both his eyes—he must have been at least half blind. For a moment I imagined his head was floating in the air, and my stomach floated up with it. But then he held the door open, and I saw that his head was attached to a body, stooped and crooked with age.

The twins moved forward with me, but the old man said, "Just the boy, please."

I stepped into the great cabin alone.

Captain Michael De Ridder was seated at an elegant desk with a quill in his hand. Open before him was a large ledger bound in brown leather with a hunk of gray ambergris—waxy stuff vomited by sperm whales, excellent for treating headache and poisoning—on the left side as a paperweight. Sunlight poured through a wall of whitish glass windows across the ship's stern. Down the center of the room was a long table that could seat ten. On the bulkhead wall hung a portrait of a pretty round-faced woman with two young children—his family, I guessed—and an embroidered sampler that read FAIR SKIES AND FOLLOWING WINDS in crooked letters. At the captain's feet slept a shaggy black dog with a head the size of a watermelon.

I chewed my thumbnail to look boyish and studied the captain carefully while he wrote, hoping to determine something of the man in his looks. Brown hair turning gray, worn loosely and pulled back under a tricorn hat. Quality linen, starched and pressed. A strong jaw in a weather-beaten face. He could be kind or cruel, wise or dull.

"Captain, may I present . . ." The servant raised shaggy eyebrows at me.

"Albert Jochims, sir," I said, taking Albertina's name for my own.

"Stowaway," he supplied helpfully.

De Ridder laid down his quill and wiped his fingers on a handkerchief.

"Thank you, Slippert. That will be all."

Slippert backed out of the cabin.

"I suppose you're our demon." De Ridder spoke in a quiet voice, but there was no mistaking his authority.

"I suppose I am, sir."

"Do you know the penalty for stowing away on a ship of the Dutch East India Company?"

"I do, sir. It's either thrown overboard with stones in my pockets or whipped to death—with salt or burning embers from the galley oven."

The captain looked amused. I couldn't imagine why. Death was no laughing matter to me.

"Tell me. What were you doing on my ship?"

I answered with care. Father was well-known. If I revealed my identity, I'd be sent back to him at the first opportunity. "I've broken no laws, sir. Well, 'cept for stowing away."

"That's a tremendous relief," De Ridder said dryly. "But I *am* curious. Why would you spend your nights cleaning and repairing my ship?"

"I'm not a thief, sir," I said. "I wanted to make myself useful."

My answer seemed to surprise De Ridder. "What else can you do?"

"I know all the sailor's knots and the names of the sails and the lines and sheets—all the ship's parts—though I've never worked 'em myself. Also, I could holystone the decks. My arms ain't too strong, but I could try to man the pumps."

"You know all the sailor's knots?" The dog laid its giant head across the captain's lap and De Ridder scratched it behind the ears. "I wonder who taught you those?" I held my tongue. "Well, Jochims, it seems a waste of life to throw you overboard. You may stay with the *Lion* for the remaining weeks until we reach Cape Town, and there you will disembark for good."

"Thank you for not executing me, sir." I nearly swooned with relief and caught myself before I did something girlish like clasp my hands to my chest.

"Indeed." He nodded. "However, you will have to be punished. Stowing away is a serious offense."

My liver turned to ice. "Yes, sir," I whispered.

"How old are you?"

"Twelve."

"I thought about as much. Twelve lashes, then. On the bottom."

It was an easy punishment, twelve lashes on the bottom. One that boys far younger than I suffered every day and then went back to playing in the streets, sore but wiser. But not one that I could take. Shirtless, I looked no different from a boy, but I could not pull down my trousers.

"No, sir! Not on the bottom. Please. I'll . . . I'll take my whipping on the back, like a man."

"You shall take your lashings on your bottom like the child you are. There's no shame in it."

"I don't need special treatment, Captain. Whip me like a man. I can take it."

"It's choice you want, is it? Then choice you shall have. Either take the lashes on your bottom or be keelhauled."

De Ridder was through with me and so had made me an offer he knew I wouldn't accept. A choice that was no choice. He pushed away his dog's head and went back to his ledger.

"Keelhauled," I whispered.

He looked up, grave-faced. "Stop this foolishness, young man. You know not what you ask."

"I beg your pardon, sir, but I do know." I described the process as the twins had told it to me.

"That's a fair account," he said. "Men die from it. Do you understand? They die of grievous wounds."

"I understand, sir. But you said I could choose my punishment." I swallowed hard. "I choose to be keelhauled."

21

Petra

"You know how to hold yer breath, Albert?"

"I—"

A pair of strong hands shoved my head into a bucket of seawater. I swallowed lungfuls, thrashing my arms and legs, until the hands yanked me up again.

"Not like that. You got to take a deep breath before you go under and then shut your mouth tight."

The hands and the voices belonged to the Gos brothers, the twins who'd brought me to the captain and who'd since decided to become my best mates now that my death was imminent.

"Ready to try again?"

I most certainly was not ready, but I couldn't tell that

to the Gos brothers while I was doubled over coughing up seawater on the fo'c'sle deck.

"Give him a thecond, brother," said the Gos with no teeth. *Goth*. Goth with the lisp and Gos with teeth.

"I—I—"

"Take your time, mate," said Goth.

"But not too much time," said his brother, squinting at the afternoon sun. "It's almost six bells. Remember, Albert, keep your arms over your face so the barnacles don't scrape your nose off."

"And keep your feet pointing down."

Gos punched Goth in the arm. "Go get him a weight!"

"A wei—?" I sputtered.

Goth slapped me unhelpfully on the back. "To tie to your feet. Tho you'll think fathter!"

Why would I want to sink faster?! With my lungs still half-drowned, I couldn't get the question out. And now Goth was tying a twenty-pound cannonball to my ankles while a growing crowd of sailors gathered around to watch.

I scanned the sun-browned faces. Bram's wasn't among them. Was he angry with me? Had he been found out and was now chained in the hold, awaiting his own punishment?

"Handth up, Al," Goth instructed. Dumbly, I obeyed, holding my arms out to the sides while he tied another rope around my waist. The rope went from me to one of the portside yards—a yard being a horizontal piece of wood that a sail hangs from—and overboard, where it disappeared under the ship, just as I would do moments from now. I cast around wild-eyed until I found the other end of the rope lashed to a yard on the starboard side. My lifeline.

"Too tight?" Goth asked, tugging on the knot.

I'd stopped coughing but couldn't speak.

Gos slapped my back again. "Don't you worry about nothing. We'll take care of you. Just keep those arms up like we said and you'll keep your nose."

A hush came over the deck. Captain De Ridder had arrived. He moved to stand at the bow so he could address the whole of the crew. Even the soldiers had been let out to witness my punishment. Sickly and hangdog as they were, I imagined I looked worse.

The *Lion* was lying to in the light wind with all her sails turned out. She was as still as she could be in the middle of an ocean.

Where's Bram?

"Lions," De Ridder said, his deep voice carrying easily in the silence. "Albert Jochims here is a confessed stowaway and must be punished for his crime. I offered him a penalty of twelve lashes, but he chose to be keelhauled instead."

A murmur went through the crowd. "That true, Al?" whispered Gos. "Why'd you do an idiot thing like that?"

"Mister Jochims," De Ridder said. "Do you wish to change your mind?"

I did. I wished to change my mind more than I wished for food or sunlight or fresh air. More than I wished for anything. Except going back to Father, which is what would happen if I was stripped and whipped.

"No, sir. I stand by my choice."

"Don't be a fool, boy!"

"Addle pate!"

"Cod's head!"

"Dullpickle!"

"Mister Jochims?" the captain asked again.

I licked salt from my lips. "Please go ahead and keelhaul me, sir."

De Ridder glared at me. "As you say. Haul him up!"

Gos stuffed a sponge tasting of rancid oil in my mouth. "It's maybe got a bit of air in it," he explained.

There was a jerk on the rope around my waist and suddenly I was dangling from the yard, the cannonball tied to my ankles threatening to sever my feet. Gos, Goth, and a mate held the end of the rope on the starboard side. Once I hit the water it would be their job to pull me from one side of the ship to the other. Too fast and I'd lose my head. Too slow and I'd drown.

Where was Bram? I felt my nostrils flare with every breath.

"Breathe before you hit the water!" yelled Gos.

He crossed his arms over his face and then touched his nose, as if I needed another reminder of the razor-sharp barnacles. I looked around again for Bram. Instead I found Clockert, still wearing his bloody apron from Barometer Piet's surgery.

"Hard over, men," De Ridder commanded. The yard swung out and now I was hanging over the sea.

"On my count," De Ridder called. "Three, two, one!"

22

Petra

Falling, falling, then a shock of cold.

And then, for a few moments, nothing. No sound, no sight. Just a rush of water and the drip of bitter oil down the back of my throat while the cannonball pulled me toward the ocean floor.

I covered my face with my arms, opened my eyes. Dark green. Falling, falling.

A snap on the rope around my waist nearly forced out the precious air I was holding. Up above, the men had started pulling. The plunge downward ceased. I lurched sideways. The *Lion*'s bottom loomed in the shadows, black and growing larger until it was all I could see.

My right leg hit the hull first. Barnacles shredded trousers and skin like paper. I ground my teeth into the sponge, desperate to scream, desperate not to open my mouth. Sliding down the side of the ship, I bounced to my back, and pain sprung afresh. I rolled onto my arms, still covering my face, still sliding down, down, and the pain bloomed.

A low fire burned in my chest, feeding on the little air I had left. I was under the ship now and could see the keel hurtling near. Too fast. At this rate, at this angle, I'd crash into it head-on.

Now, out of the corner of my eye, I saw another dark shape emerge, a long black shadow cutting through the water. I knew that sharks always followed ships, lured by the garbage left in their wake. This one must have scented my blood. Others wouldn't be far behind.

The keel was just a few feet away, but the shark would reach me first. I closed my eyes—

A hand took hold of my wrist. Bram's hand! *He* was the dark shape. He grabbed my other wrist and put both my hands on his shoulders, then twisted so I clung to his back. Bram dove, leading us down and away from the keel. How he swam against the pull of the rope, against the weight of the iron ball, I shall never know, but somehow Bram's legs were strong enough to keep us both away from the barnacles. We passed under the keel by inches and then passed the rest of the bottom of the hull with room to spare. The fire raged in my lungs, and at last we rose up, toward the light, toward air. Just before we broke the surface of the water, Bram twisted away from me and disappeared.

23

Bram

"Cut him down!"

"Is he dead?"

"Make way!"

As all eyes was on Petra, I climbed up the aft portside rigging without getting smoked. She hung from the starboard yard, limp as a fish. With all the blood dripping off her, she looked dead but for her chest, which was pumping up and down. The Gos twins was working to cut her loose. I hung back where no one was looking. Soon as I saw Petra was fit, I'd go below and get dry.

Clockert was at her now. He tore open one of her sleeves. Seemed like there was more blood than skin left. Me, I didn't have a scratch. Once I had a hold of Petra, 'twas simple enough to keep us both off the barnacles. 'Twasn't anything to crow about. Most sailors couldn't swim—they figured it's better to meet your maker quick than float around waiting to be shark supper. But I'd grown up fishing and could swim as easy as I could walk. And I could hold my breath for three minutes, which was, now that I think of it, maybe something to crow about.

Clockert must've not liked the look of Petra, because he was having the Gos boys carry her down to the sick bay. I couldn't tell if she was passed out or awake. Her eyes was shut and her skin was a queer gray color. She'd kept her face off the barnacles and all her parts seemed to be attached, but anyone could tell she was badly done in just the same.

I headed down an aft hatch, away from the crowds, to change into some dry duds in the carpenter's cabin. I was just tying the strings on my trousers when Pa came in.

"Didn't see you at the boy's keelhauling," he said.

"I don't much go in for that kind of thing," I told him.

He eyed me. Reached out a hand and picked up my braid, which was dripping down my back.

"Why's your hair wet, Bram?"

'Twas no use lying. He'd know it. "I helped Jochims over the keel."

Pa nodded like he thought it was a good idea I made sure a boy got to keep his head on. "You hurt?"

"Nah," I said.

"Anyone see you?"

"No, Pa. I was careful."

"All right then."

I said something about paintwork and instead went aft to Clockert's cabin. He was in there with Petra, alone except for Barometer Piet, who was snoring behind the curtain.

She was slumped over in a chair. Her shirt was pushed off one shoulder, which was scraped up pretty bad, as was both arms and one leg.

"Not now, Broen," Clockert said.

"I thought maybe you could use a hand, master," I said.

"Now that you mention it, my assistant seems to have disappeared yet again, and I could benefit from your services. Bring me that pot of ointment from the table, please, whilst I cut away Mister Jochims's clothes." Clockert held up a pair of scissors.

"No, don't! You can't do that!"

"I beg your pardon?"

"Only it's just—see how he's squirming? Those are probably his only clothes, him being a stowaway and all. If you cut 'em off, what'll he wear?"

"Please, master," Petra croaked. "He's right."

Clockert looked back and forth at me and Petra like we was a couple of lunatics, but he shrugged.

"As you wish. If you prefer to convalesce in wet rags, far be it from me to stop you, Mister Jochims."

Petra slumped over again while Clockert rolled up her trousers and I brought over the pot of ointment.

"Mister Jochims, may I present Bram Broen, carpenter's mate. He's going to hold your hand steady whilst I sew your arm. Mister Broen, may I present Albert Jochims."

I picked up Petra's hand like 'twas made of china. "How now, Jochims?"

Petra lifted her head an inch. "Fair to middling, all things considered, Broen."

We stayed like that for some time, me holding parts of Petra steady while Clockert sewed or smeared on some of his medicines. Every so often, Clockert'd give her some brandy. After the first few sips, she swigged it like a sailor. When he was done, Clockert bandaged her arms and legs so's they looked like cocoons.

"Well, Jochims, you bore your punishment like a man," Clockert said, helping her to her feet. "Go have a rest next to Barometer Piet."

24

Petra

I woke in daylight, but I knew not the time. Behind the curtain in Clockert's office, I lay on a cot next to Barometer Piet, who was sleeping, though his color looked a shade less gray than it had on the surgeon's table. As for me, I felt surprisingly well. My clothes were dry, and my head, limbs, and nose were all in their proper places. So long as I kept perfectly still, the pain from my wounds was tolerable, if only just.

Moving was another matter. When I sat up it felt as though my bandaged shoulder brushed hot coals instead of canvas. I rolled the torn leg of my trousers over my knee so it wouldn't rub against the bandage on my leg, and did the same with my sleeves. Clockert must have changed my dressings while I slept, for they were fresh.

Slowly, I stood. I was reminded of our neighbor Ewout Tchoe. At ninety-two, he was the oldest man in Amsterdam, the oldest man anyone could remember. Ancient Ewout Tchoe moved faster than I.

To my surprise, standing felt more comfortable than sitting or lying down, with nothing chafing my raw skin. I shuffled past the curtain. Clockert was at his desk with three books open. There was no sign of the unfortunate Krause.

"Pardon me, master, may I come in?"

"Ah! It's our very own Lazarus. Welcome back to the living, sir. You've been away for two nights and a day. It's Saturday morning."

"Have I really been asleep all that time?"

"You have. Barometer Piet was most impressed. By your wounds and by your slumber. Unlike you, he seems to prefer being awake during the night watches."

Which accounted for the dark shadows under Clockert's eyes.

"Thank you for looking after me, master. And for the fresh dressing," I said, gently lifting an arm.

"Your leg bled for quite some time, but it's stopped now."

My leg? Had the surgeon noticed anything else about me when he changed my bandages? His manner toward me seemed natural enough, but how could I be certain?

"You look tolerably well now, young man. Off you go

to your cabin or your work or whatever it is you plan to do with yourself." With a wave of dismissal, Clockert returned to his reading. But I remained standing in his doorway for a rather long awkward minute.

"Yes, well, about that." I cleared my throat. "About working—"

Clockert slammed one of his books shut. "Exactly how much of my spirits have you drunk?"

"Me, sir? Not a drop!"

"Stolen, then. To sell off for your own selfish profit."

"Not a bottle. On my honor."

Clockert lifted an eyebrow.

"I know as a stowaway I appear to have no honor whatsoever, sir—" *Mind your speech, Petra! Talk like a common boy.* "But I got some, and I swear I never touched your spirits. Never once."

"I have counted the bottles and four have been taken."

"Not by me, sir." I'd seen Krause take the storeroom key from Clockert's drawer and steal the bottles, but I'd not be an informer.

"In that case, why do you remain here, if not to confess your crimes?"

"I just thought, master, maybe you needed help in the sick bay?"

"Help from whom?"

"From me, sir. I been watching you these last months, and—"

"No." Clockert returned to one of his remaining open books.

"No?"

"I already have one useless boy in my service. I've no need of two."

"I can read, sir. And write."

"In Latin?" Clockert challenged.

"Only Dutch. And a little English," I admitted. "But I can sew. I can cook too, if you need some medicine brewed up."

"An interesting assortment of skills for an ordinary young man," Clockert observed.

"Yes—*aye*, well, my mother was a housekeeper, sir, and I was with her when she did her work."

"A housekeeper with a son who reads and writes in two languages?"

I felt my face flush. My story was fast becoming as ridiculous as my grammar. I was no play actor. Better to stay close to the truth.

"I meant a *fine* housekeeper," I said in my usual accent. "My mother was an English housewife with fine skills in the house."

"I see," Clockert said. And I was very much afraid that he did. But he dropped the line of questioning and surprised me instead. "Very well. Go check on Pietersen. Help him with the chamber pot if he needs it. Change his bandage and apply the proper plaster on the wound, which, if you've been spying on me as much as you claim, you should know how to make by now. Then cut new bandages from fresh linen. Tidy my sick room and sharpen the knives I left on the table. I noticed during the surgery my scalpel was dull—more's the pity for poor Pietersen. When you've finished those tasks, you may bring me my dinner."

"As you wish, sir."

I felt an unfamiliar smile break across my face, though the thought of helping Barometer Piet with the chamber pot gave me pause. But Tina had never shied away from such things, not when patients, male or female, needed her help. I resolved to follow her example.

Slowly, painfully, I crept my way through each of the tasks Clockert had assigned me. The surgeon dismissed me at the end of the afternoon watch, by which time I was thoroughly exhausted. But with the taste of happiness fresh on my tongue, the chance to see blue sky in the remaining hour before twilight was irresistible.

I stood amidships with my back to the rail and pulled off my cap, then untied my hair so the gentle breeze could blow the strands from my face. The air blew in puffs and the sea had a swell to it that propelled the ship in long, heaving rolls, but the men went about their work as comfortably as if they were on dry land. They swarmed the deck like a colony of spiders preparing for an onslaught of flies. There were men touching up paintwork, men splicing and weaving rope, men repairing sails, their needles moving as fast as Albertina's in the years before her fingers stiffened. A few enjoyed moments of leisure in the fading sunlight, which they spent scrawling in journals or whittling scraps of wood into exotic animals. Goats roamed and chickens staggered, while aft on the poop deck a black-and-white sow gulped slops from a trough. Behind me in the waist, Kosnik the giant smith was roasting iron in the forge, while next to him Jaya the cooper hammered strips of bent wood into a barrel. The captain was on the quarterdeck with Oak by his side. Even seated, the great dog's head reached past De Ridder's waist. The beast seemed to relish the sea spray that doused his face. He shook salt water from his furry cheeks along with long strands of drool from his black lips.

And there it was at last: the crow's nest. High up in the clouds, a lookout rested his elbows on the rail and scanned the horizon with a spyglass.

Every line was in its place, but the sails flapped in the light wind. Across from me, a sailor leaned over the rail, measuring the speed of the ship under Van Plaes's supervision. He unspooled a length of knotted rope from a wooden reel and let it trail in the water, counting the number of knots that passed during the time it took for sand to run from one end of a minute glass to the other. The first mate recorded the speed in the ship's log.

"Just two knots, Captain!" Van Plaes reported.

"Thank you, Mister Van Plaes." The captain turned his weather-beaten face to the bosun. "Mister Grof, the wind here is not what we would wish it to be. Tell the men to prepare to jibe." Before Grof had begun to repeat the order to change course, the men were already scrambling up the rigging to trim the sails.

A shadow fell over me. "Bram Broen," said a slender black-eyed boy. "We met earlier in Clockert's cabin."

"Albert Jochims," I said solemnly. "I believe we met even earlier than that, somewhere between the rail and the keel, if I'm not mistaken."

"You must have me mixed up with someone else, mate. I never go swimming in August."

I squeezed Bram's hand in thanks and he squeezed mine back.

"We was all quite *surprised* by your arrival in sick bay," he said.

"No more than I," I assured him.

Bram leaned down and spoke into my ear. "All of it. Now, please."

I relayed all that had happened from the moment I entered the captain's cabin—leaving out the keelhauling, which he knew as well as I. When I described how I convinced Clockert to take me on, Bram whistled.

"So you're all set then," he said. "And since you're a boy, you can land in Batavia with the rest of us and sail somewheres else, as you please."

"Nay." I frowned. "The captain says I must disembark for good in Cape Town."

"That won't do," Bram said. "Cape Town's nothing but a few tents and hovels. If Hottentots don't skin you alive, wild animals will. And if the wild animals leave you alone, a sickness'll carry you off. It's right unhealthful and no place to live."

I pictured dark men with big machetes and pointed teeth like Happy Jan's. "Then I shall board the very next ship that stops there and go where it takes me."

"Even if it takes you to Holland?"

I wouldn't let it come to that. Just as Bram was proving himself with hard work, I would prove myself indispensable as surgeon's mate so that De Ridder would allow young Albert Jochims to stay on.

As if he could see into my mind, Bram said, "Did the captain say anything about me when you was in his cabin?"

"Not a word," I assured him. "He said only that he guessed I was the demon who repaired sails and whipped lines in the night, and I admitted as much. But he didn't ask about the oakum or the staves and I expect he still believes it all came from you."

"I hope you're right. I'll have to make the stuff myself now so no one'll catch on."

"I'll help you. We can do it at night."

A sailor dumped a bucket over the rail and Bram and

I stood in unhappy silence watching the sharks devour the slops.

"Everyone's talking about how you saved Barometer Piet's life," he said at last.

"I don't know what I was thinking. One minute I was behind the wall, quiet as you please, and the next I was over and out."

"You're lucky 'twas Piet you saved."

"Why is that?"

"Piet's a favorite on board. He knows the sea as well as any man alive and he can always tell when a storm's coming. That's a rare valuable talent on a ship."

And it explained the nickname, a barometer being the instrument that measures the changes in air pressure that precede a storm. "How can he tell a storm is coming?" I asked.

Bram shrugged. "He says he can feel it in the fingers of his left hand."

I was familiar with Barometer Piet's left hand, having washed it that afternoon. It had a thumb and an index finger. The other digits were missing.

"My pa says you can bunk and mess with us," Bram said. "He cleared it with the captain."

I hadn't considered that I would no longer have to steal food or sleep in the hold. Joining Bram and Paulus's mess sounded like dear luxury.

"Al!"

The Gos brothers joined us. Gos raised his hand to slap me on the back but stopped himself when I flinched.

"Good to thee you up and about," Goth said. "How're you coming along?"

"Well enough," I said. "Thank you for your help with the ke-keelhauling."

" 'Twas the least we could do after treating you so rough before." The twins had sheepish looks on their spotted faces. "Me and my brother were a couple of louts to tell it real. But we've come to say sorry. After what you did for Barometer Piet, we got together with some of the crew and rounded up some gear. Seeing as how you're a stowaway and all, we figured you could use a few things. No offense meant, of course."

"None taken," I said, making an effort to add what I hoped was a masculine heft to my voice.

Gos handed me a tarred canvas ditty bag, and I untied the drawstring. Inside was a wood cup and spoon, some sewing supplies, a watertight pouch of tobacco, and a stone bottle of gin.

I swallowed the lump that had swelled in my throat. "This is too much. I can't possibly repay—"

"Don't go crying like a girl now," Goth said, making my lump double in size from fear. "Think of it ath a welcome aboard from your new mateth."

"Albert Jochims!" called Louis Cheval from across the deck, pronouncing my name in the French fashion.

Louis trotted up to us, smiling. "'Ello, Albert Jochims. I am 'appy to see you are alive. Are you French like your name?"

"I'm afraid not," I said, relieved that Louis seemed not to recognize his old hat on my head. *"Mais je parle français très bien."*

Louis looked aghast. "Please, Albert, never do that again. Your French is too 'orrible. But we can be friends anyway." Turning to Bram, he said, *"Monsieur* Bram, I 'ave a message for you from the captain."

"Aye?" Bram said.

" 'E would like you to join 'im for dinner tomorrow."

25

Bram

'Twas usual for De Ridder to sup with his officers, and most days he added a crewman or two, picked 'cause they did something extra. Today that crewman was me. But I was asking myself, was the something extra hiding a stowaway or steaming all those barrels?

I could hardly keep my eyes open after downing what must've been a gallon of wine. With the ship's beer stores long drunk, I was used to just three little cups of gin a day. Plus all the slimy water I could drink. 'Twas good to have all your teeth, 'cause they kept the water worms from going down your throat, though the scum did turn 'em green. Come to think of it, the water at the captain's table was hardly wormy at all. Seemed the officers got a better class of bever than we crew.

The captain's table was something to behold. Each man had his own plate and we drank out of glasses so fine I feared I might snap mine in two if I held it too tight. Even the salt came in a fancy silver pot.

Every couple of minutes the captain would jump up and say, "Why, gentlemen, we can't have you looking low! Allow me to refill your glasses." Well, no wonder our glasses needed refilling when every cove at the table felt like it was his duty to offer a toast—or three—to Holland, to wives and sisters at home, or to "catching a fish," which was another way of saying taking a Spanish galleon loaded with treasure. The law said if two nations was at war, 'twas fair for the ship of one country to plunder the ship of another. Now, my mind couldn't work out the difference between this and what pirates do, but I wouldn't say no to my share of the purse.

I got my toast out of the way early on: "To fair skies and following seas!" Petra'd told me that's what the letters spelled on the fancy needlework that hung on the captain's wall, and I couldn't think of anything better.

The rule was that no man at the captain's table could speak without the captain speaking to him first, and I was glad of it, since I had no idea what to say to all those officers and high-ups. When De Ridder finally called on me, the glazed goose in my belly turned to stone.

"Mister Broen. I've seen you hard at work these last

weeks. Well done." I perked up a bit. Maybe 'twas making the barrels and not hiding Petra that got me invited. "Your efforts at repairing the rigging were quite impressive."

"Well, sir, my mother's people was fishermen, so I know a fair bit about rigging." During the years Pa was at sea, which was most of my life, I'd lived with my ma and her family on Java.

"Were they?" he said. "And do you know how to swim?"

"I do, sir."

"Such a useful skill," boomed Isaack Van Swalme, the VOC's rep and the most important cove on the ship. Nary a hair graced the man's head, but he made up for it with a white mustache that swooped down from his upper lip under his cheeks and up to his temples like a topsy-turvy heart. Plus two blobs of beard stuck on his chin like fat cotton balls. The whole effect was ridiculous, if anyone asked me, which they didn't. "Did you dive for crustaceans or was it just nets and boats?" The merchant's voice seemed to float over the table from a league away.

"We did both, sir."

"Ever find a pearl, Bram?" Midshipman Johann Majoor leaned in like it was time for dessert, which, I'm sorry to say, it wasn't. 'Twas the first time he'd spoken to me like a mate. He was an officer, as was his right by high birth, and I was crew and always would be. The wall between us didn't allow for friendly conversation.

"Just little gray ones." Majoor looked let down, so I

said, "But my cousin found one once as big as his thumbnail." I didn't tell him that nine people ate for a month thanks to that pearl.

"Pearl fishing is an unreliable business," said Van Swalme, cotton balls bobbing while he chewed.

"I'm sure you can tell us a better one," said Clockert.

Van Swalme pegged the doctor with a stern eye. "I most certainly can, gentlemen. African slaves."

A murmur went round the table.

"Have you experience in the industry?" the captain asked.

"I do not," said Van Swalme, mopping up red sauce from his plate with a piece of gooseflesh and stuffing it into his mouth. "But I mean to. It's the only form of private trade permitted by the Dutch West India Company and as such has none of the bureaucracy we merchants suffer in the East. New Netherland has a dire need of slave labor—Stuyvesant is practically begging for hands to build his fortresses and till his fields in New Amsterdam. A smart man can fill a ship in African Angola with four hundred slaves at fifty-five florins a head and unload them in the Caribbean for two hundred eighty. Then he sails up to New Amsterdam to fill his hold with lumber and skins for the journey back to Europe and repeats the process until he retires in comfort."

I didn't like this talk of slavery. I'd seen too much of it on Java, and if I went back there, my own life would be almost near as bad. But Clockert was like a dog after a bone.

"Fascinating," he said. "Mister Van Assendorp, I believe you've spent some time on slave ships, have you not?"

"I have," said the commander of soldiers. His white scar stood out on his weathered face like a crescent moon in a dirty sky.

"What do you think of *Monsieur* Van Swalme's assertions that slavery is our next growth industry?" Clockert asked.

"I wouldn't presume to guess, sir," Van Assendorp said. "Mister Van Swalme is a successful gentleman merchant. I'm only a soldier."

"What was it like, Commander? Is it true the slaves eat their own young?" It had to be the wine that made Majoor bold enough to ask, because any dolt should know that a slave ship had to be the closest thing to hell on earth or sea.

"The Africans are devil worshipers," said that cod's head Van Swalme.

"There isn't a man, woman, or child among them that isn't spending every waking second trying to kill himself rather than be a slave," Van Assendorp said. "The crew spend much of their time trying to prevent suicide."

Those slaves knew what was in store for 'em and they'd rather be dead. I couldn't say I'd feel otherwise if I was in their place.

"My very point indeed," said Van Swalme. "Murder and suicide are mortal sins."

"As is the wasting of good food," said the captain, who clearly had no liking for the direction the parley had taken. "Slippert!"

The steward poked his whiskered face around the door. "Sir?"

"More goose, please."

"Right away, sir." Slippert backed out of the cabin.

"An excellent dinner, Captain." The cotton balls on Van Swalme's chin was stained blood red from the duck sauce. "You are fortunate in Happy Jan."

"Thank you, Isaack. Yes, Jan joined me two voyages ago in Cape Town. He had tired of being a supplier in the black trade and desired a fresh beginning. I am fortunate in much of my crew. Van Plaes has sailed with me since I was first mate and he a midshipman on the *Full Moon*."

"Sheep will always follow a strong shepherd," said Van Swalme.

"Yes, well, I know little about sheep, but it has been my experience that loyalty follows respect, and respect must be mutual," the captain said.

The recipe works 'til you add three million florins to the pot. I was sober now but wished I wasn't. My head was crammed with pictures of dead African slaves and of Captain De Ridder, marooned by his greedy crew on some lonely island with a one-shot pistol and a sack of salt pork and dried peas.

26

Petra

The sun had peaked when my new messmates and I ate brown beans and salt cod from a shared bowl in the waist. The day was hellishly warm, and the crew sprawled on the deck, stockings and jackets off, sweating through their shirts and trousers. I felt no better with my wounds stinging and my bandages growing damp. Poor Bram. It must have been hotter still in the captain's cabin where he was supping.

Jeronimo Lobo the gunner, who wore his shabby sailor's jacket like an aristocrat's frock coat, raised his cup. "To our new mate, Albert Jochims!"

Paulus tapped Jaya's cup with his own, and as one, they all took a swig of gin. I followed and gagged on the fire, but it was better than slimy green water.

I lifted a ship's biscuit to my mouth, when Lobo shot out a hand to stop me. "Like this," he said. He rapped the biscuit on the deck and small insects scurried out. "Tastes better without the weevils." He grinned, giving me an opportunity to appreciate white teeth whose shine matched the gleam of his gold earrings.

The decks were crowded with men seeking fresh air in the hot weather. German, Swedish, Polish, French, Flemish, Portuguese, and Malaysian mixed with Dutch to create a seafaring lingo that was somehow understandable to everyone on board, although not, as yet, to me.

Behind our group, the Polish trio—the smith, the gun maker, and the sword keeper—were eating together. I knew them from Bram's drawings. The sword keeper was a small wiry man who could boast of having all his teeth but no tongue since he lost his in a bar fight in Tangiers. He approached our group and waited for the men to notice him. When they did, the sword keeper removed a leather cloth from inside his jacket and slowly unwrapped it to reveal a gleaming new short knife. Why the knife was called "short" was beyond me, but all sailors carried them and called them so. The single-edged blade was about six inches long and blunt at the end, with its handle wrapped in twine for a good grip. To my surprise, the sword keeper bowed and presented it to me.

"He says it is having good balance with sharp edge that cuts one hundred sharks to pieces," Kosnik the enormous smith said in passable Dutch. I had to wonder how the tongueless sword keeper managed to communicate all that to his mate.

Lobo took the knife from me and tapped another biscuit on the deck. When the weevils scurried out, he sliced one clean in half.

"She's beautiful," I said to the sword keeper, taking back the knife. "I shall use it well." The knife would be infinitely useful. I was already thinking about the sheath I would make so that I could wear it on my hip as the crew did theirs.

The sword keeper crossed his fists over his heart. The letters tattooed on his knuckles spelled ANGELIKA.

After the sword keeper rejoined his mates, Lobo said, "All right, Jochims, out with it."

"Out with what?" I said, my mind clouded with gin and heat.

Little Louis Cheval plunked down next to me. "'Ow did you stow away? *Why* did you stow away? And 'ow did you not to get caught for three months?"

The eyes of all my new messmates were on me, as well as those of a good portion of the other men on the fo'c'sle. Once again, I decided the truth—even a partial one—was easier to tell than a lie.

"I stowed away because of a personal matter, gentlemen, and I'm sorry I can't say more than that except I'm not in any trouble with the law—"

"You're the only one here, then," said Lobo, and the others laughed.

"I hid in the hold," I continued, "and only came out at night for food. Happy Jan caught me once, but I told him I was Van Swalme's boy and he let me go."

"You want to steer clear of 'appy Jan for a while," Louis advised. "'E won't like being tricked."

"Louis's right," Paulus said, a frown on his freckled face. "Don't cross Happy Jan. The cove made slaves of his own people."

"How?"

"When he live in Angola, Happy Jan capture other Africans and sell to slave traders for money." Jaya leaned over and spit betel juice through the rail. "Keep far from him. A man such as this would sell his own mother."

I vowed that I would.

"It seems you did more at night than take food from the galley," Lobo said, changing the subject.

"I can't deny it." I felt myself blush. "It was I who made all the mischief on board, cobbling sails and sharpening swords. I'm sorry if I put anyone out."

"No, no. We are grateful. You did much work for many of us," Jaya said. "Tell us. Was it also you who made my staves?"

"Not I, sir," I said, hoping my face didn't look as hot as it felt. "I'd no part in your staves."

"That was Bram, remember, Jaya?" Paulus said. "Now,

Jochims, you left out the best parts of your story: How'd you come aboard and why'd you come out?"

"I came aboard with the chickens," I admitted, grateful to Paulus for turning the conversation from my secret activities, for I was half sure he suspected me of helping Bram. "And I came out because the sailor who carried me lay gutted on Clockert's table and needed my help. It was only fair, gentlemen."

The sailors relished the idea that Barometer Piet had smuggled me on board without knowing it and that I in turn had found a way to repay him.

"Welcome to the sea, *Monsieur* Jochims," said Louis, raising his cup. "A merry life and a short one!"

"Longest liver takes all!" offered Lobo.

All the sailors nearby cheered and slapped the deck. Except for Kaspar Krause, who huddled in a corner staring out to sea.

Paulus followed the direction of my gaze. "He's been demoted, you know."

"Krause?"

"Aye. Our surgeon's mate is just another ordinary seaman now." He scanned the nearest mast to the top, barely visible in the relentless glare of the afternoon sun. "Hope he has a good grip."

I thought the only good grip Krause had was on a bottle. "I didn't mean—"

"No one says you did, Jochims. A ship has no room

for lubbers," said Jaya in a voice loud enough to carry to Krause's corner. I knew there was nothing the men hated more than a lazy mate.

Krause pushed himself up and shuffled to the nearest hatch.

"Who's ready for a swim!" shouted a sailor.

"Aye to that, *amigo!*" Lobo leaped to his feet.

Within moments, shirts and breeches went flying.

"I thought the men couldn't swim," I squeaked. "And what about sharks?"

"No need to worry," Paulus said, taking off his tool belt. "The men'll rig a sail in the water for a little pool. And they'll tie up the edges so sharks can't get in."

Stamp my vitals, Bram's father was unlacing his trousers!

Worse, Lobo extended his hand to me, naked but for the tattoos on his— "Come on, Jochims! Have a swim."

27

Petra

I stumbled to the hold as fast as my injuries would allow and sat down heavily on a barrel. Mortification was the least of my worries. What if the men had insisted I swim with them? I couldn't afford to arouse even the slightest suspicion that I was a girl, for then I would certainly be sent back to Father.

I found bolts of linen stored in the corner of the main hold. Using my new short knife, I cut a generous swath and then tore that into long strips. A quick glance up the hatch to make sure no one was coming, and I pulled off my shirt.

I wound the linen around my torso, stopping well below the bandage on my shoulder so that Clockert wouldn't see the bindings when he changed my dressing. My body hadn't started to soften, but it could at any time and I would take no chance of being found out. I pulled the fabric tighter with each circle until it hurt to take a full breath. Only a few months ago I'd begged Albertina for my first corset and been angry when she said it was too soon. I'd wept then over not being womanly enough. Now I wept because I was too womanly.

Tina, what would you say if you could see me?

I'd say you're doin' what needs to be done, Petje. Like always.

⁓

Four days after the keelhauling, I was feeling somewhat less stiff and achy. I left for the sick bay before dawn while the early watch were holystoning the decks, and Bram and Paulus were somehow sleeping through the racket.

Barometer Piet was the only patient in the infirmary.

"There's my boy!" Piet croaked when he saw me. "I thought you was Saint Nicholas the Wonderworker come to save me, but my mates told me different."

The leathery sailor was nearly delirious with thirst and his bandage was soaked yellowy red.

"How are you feeling, Piet?" I helped him sip some barley water. It was the first time he'd been up to conversation since his surgery.

"Never better now that I know you and me is squared. We *is* squared, ain't we?"

"Perfectly." I mopped his face with a cool wet cloth. "Do you think you could take some broth?"

Piet winced. "Later, sonny. For now, I want to hear how it was I stowed you away."

I pulled up a stool and told Barometer Piet how I'd wedged myself among the birdcages.

"Lobo said it got heavy! Remember how it swayed—"

"I nearly died of fright thinking I'd fall straight into the sea!"

We laughed together until Barometer Piet stopped suddenly and narrowed his wrinkled eyes at me. "So that fancy gentleman looking for his lost child . . . he musta been . . ."

My head went numb. How could I have forgotten that Barometer Piet and Lobo had met Father!

"A coincidence—"

"He said he was missing . . ." Barometer Piet continued, thinking out loud, "a *daughter*. With yellow hair . . ."

We stared at each other. I took a deep breath and felt the linen tighten around my chest. How much did Piet suspect? "I don't know that man. Or his daughter. I'm Albert Jochims," I said firmly.

A long moment of silence passed before Barometer Piet nodded his grizzled head. "A pleasure to make your acquaintance, Albert."

Clockert arrived then, his eyes red-rimmed and his clothes more rumpled than usual. His hair looked as if rats had been at war in it all night long.

"Mister Pietersen. I'm happy you are still with us, seeing as how it was not a foregone conclusion. Jochims, what have you to say about our patient?"

I stood to make my report, determined to impress the surgeon. "Good morning, sir. Barometer Piet is doing well. I believe—"

"Prithee halt." Clockert held up a hand. "Now that you are speaking, I realize I do not care to hear what you have to say. I shall examine the patient myself."

He placed a hand on Barometer Piet's forehead. "A moderate fever, as to be expected." Looked under his eyelids. "Clear." Lifted the bandage. "A laudable pus. Well, Mister Pietersen, your recovery seems to be proceeding apace. Later I shall bleed you to draw down the ill humors that oppress your liver and spleen. For now, my assistant shall administer a fresh plaster and redress your wound."

"Thankee, master," Barometer Piet said, suddenly looking rather small and old.

I took care of Barometer Piet and went up to the fo'c'sle to breakfast. The sky was heavy and gray, with a new bite of cold in the air. After his wine-soaked dinner yesterday, Bram couldn't stomach his morning ration of porridge.

"Take it," he said to me. "I can't look at it."

"Nor I," I said, turning away from the sodden lump.

"You'd be doing him a favor, Jochims," Lobo said. "He'll get flogged for wasting food."

I ate the porridge. Bram had saved my life twice—now we were even.

"You're new to the sea, Jochims. It's no wonder you don't know bow from stern," Paulus said. "But we're your messmates, so if you've got any questions, fire away."

As it happened, I did have a question.

"Jochims?" Paulus asked.

It was a bit awkward to put into words.

"I . . . er . . . that is, I was wondering . . ."

"Out with it, boy," Jaya said not ungently.

"Well, it's about the head."

"Your head?" Paulus asked.

"No, not *my* head," I said, "*the* head." The head was a privy box at the bow of the ship that the crew used when they had needs that couldn't be relieved over the rail. It had a hole in the top and was set on grating that was open to the sea below.

"You mean the *seat of ease*?" Lobo said.

"The *jardine*?" said Jaya.

"The *beak*?" said Bram, looking perkier.

I felt my face flush.

"You need to know how to use the head?" Paulus asked, putting an end to the teasing, I hoped.

"I know how to use it, thank you. What I don't understand is why there's a tremendously long thick rope running through the hole in the seat and down into the water."

"You mean the butt-broom?" Bram wheezed, laughing so hard he rolled on the deck.

"The *what*?"

"The butt-broom," Jaya said, gold earrings bobbing merrily.

"Do you mean to say that the crew uses that coarse rope to wipe their bottoms?" The whole ship must be rife with hemorrhoids!

"Next time you're there, pull the rope through the box," Paulus said, giving the others a stern look that cut off their guffaws. "The end that drags in the sea? It's got long, *soft* fringe at the end, like a mop. *That's* the part you use for wiping."

"Well. That's another matter, then," I said, too primly for any boy.

Bram shot me a look, but the rest of them dissolved into laughter again.

⁓

I returned to the sick bay, where Clockert was tending to his first patient of the day, Van Swalme's serving boy, Tixfor, who couldn't stop scratching himself.

"It doesn't take a medicine man to see that you're suffering from *pediculosis capitis,* or an infestation of Phthiraptera." Seeing Tixfor's bewildered expression, he sighed. "The common head louse."

While Clockert spoke, one of the creatures actually

crawled out from Tixfor's black hair and across his temple to bury itself behind his ear. Tixfor twitched.

"How can I make 'em go away, sir?"

"It's nothing a razor won't cure," Clockert said. "Jochims, shave this boy's head, please."

"Oh, no, master!" Tixfor exclaimed, his blue eyes widening with alarm. "It took me my whole life to grow this tail." He clutched his meager braid with both hands. "You can't cut it off!"

Clockert looked down his nose at the tormented young man. "In that case, you must douse your head in the piss barrel. And while you're at it, wash your clothes as well. Urine," he explained to me, "is an excellent delouser and purifier. For future reference, you'll find the barrel next to the mainmast on the upper deck. Feel free to add to it should the need arise. The other men do."

"Yes, sir." *Butt-brooms and piss barrels. What next? Vomitoriums?*

Shortly after the start of the afternoon watch, Jaya came to visit Barometer Piet. I was in the sick bay labeling medicine jars, but I could hear their conversation through the curtain.

"How are you, my brother?" Jaya said.

Barometer Piet grunted and I heard rustling. I assumed he was trying to sit up. "Never better, mate. Doc Clock bled me near dry this morning and I feel like a newborn babe."

"I am glad to hear it. We worried." Jaya spit betel juice into his cup.

"I bet you did," Piet said, with a note of some extra meaning in his tone.

Jaya lowered his voice. "There is work to do. Do you think you will be down long?"

"Don't you worry, mate," Piet said at half his usual volume. "If anything goes amiss, it'll be the wind and the weather, not Barometer Piet. I never lacked for guts before and I don't now, even with half my insides gone."

"That is what I said to them. But you know Van Assendorp," Jaya said.

"Tell the commander to take his hemming and hawing and shove 'em where the sun don't shine. Barometer Piet'll outlive him and his ten bastard kids—even with half a belly and seven fingers."

"I shall give your good wishes to our brothers," Jaya chuckled, stepping into the sick bay.

"With all due respect!" Barometer Piet called after him.

When Jaya had gone, I stuck my head through the doorway. "Are you all right, Piet?"

Barometer Piet was propped up in bed, pale-faced. He forced a grin and then collapsed back onto his cot. "Between you and me, I'm all stoved up. Feels like there's barnacles where my old ribs used to be."

"Let me get you a draught."

"Brandy?" Piet asked hopefully.

"Better than brandy. Laudanum."

I spooned the bitter opium tincture into his mouth and Barometer Piet sighed. "That's better. I can feel it working already."

In fact, it was too soon to take effect, but I was glad the idea of the medicine gave him comfort. I sat by Barometer Piet's side and watched his breathing grow easier. Just before he drifted into a deep sleep, he opened an eye at me.

"We ain't square, you know. I carried you down to the bowels of hell, where you work all hours, the food's lousy, and the pay's worse. You saved my life. We won't be square 'til I save yours."

28

Petra

"You busy?" Bram asked.

I looked up from the pigskin I was using to practice stitches, pigskin being the material on board closest to human flesh. Bram's face was black with powder from exercising the guns. Clockert and I didn't join in these drills, since in the event of battle we'd be stationed below, repairing the wounded. When weather permitted, all hands practiced rolling the four-thousand-pound cannons from their braces and loading them with powder and shot. The price of powder was too dear to fire the guns every day, but the captain sometimes ordered the men to fire on Sundays. What better way to honor the Lord than with a deafening explosion of artillery?

"Why?" I asked.

"You never did climb the mast. And," he added in a low voice, "We need to talk."

I'd been at my station through two watches already, but fatigue vanished in an instant. This was the moment I'd worked for all those weeks in the gymnasium. I glanced at Clockert for permission. Ten days after the keelhauling, my stiches were out and the wounds were healing nicely.

"Try not to fall," he said.

Bram and I climbed to the waist, where we found Louis Cheval and two sailors urinating over the rail.

"'Ave a pee with us, Albert!" Louis called.

"Thank you, Louis, but I've no need," I said.

"Baptize the ocean, Jochims," said one of the sailors. "It's the Lord's day."

I shot a worried glance at Bram.

"Sorry, mates," he said. "We've got business."

He led me to the fo'c'sle.

"Bram," I said under my breath.

"Forget it. They was just joking around."

This time.

I craned my neck to gaze to the top of the foremast, which suddenly looked two hundred feet tall at least, and decided that for the moment I had worse problems than being female. It'd been some time since I'd practiced climbing. Would my muscles know what to do?

The mast had once been the trunk of a great fir tree

and was so thick at the bottom that I could not have circled it with my arms. A grid of ropes stretched from the rail to a lookout platform halfway up and then to a second platform three-quarters of the way up. From there, more rope went to the yard that held the sails near the very top of the mast.

"You remember the first part," Bram said, taking hold of a rope. "You just climb it like a ladder."

I did remember the first part, and it wasn't like a ladder. Ladders didn't give way when a person stepped on them. Nor did they sway in a wild alarming fashion each time the ship crested a wave. But I hadn't spent weeks practicing in the hold to quit now.

Bram swung himself up, balancing on cordage as naturally as a monkey on a branch. I clambered onto the rail, awkward as a pig in a ballroom.

"It's best if you don't stop. Or look down," Bram advised.

My gut lurched with the motion of the ship. I tugged my hat over my ears, set my teeth, and began to climb.

Bram stayed two steps ahead of me, although I suspected he could have made it to the top, down, and up again in the time it took me to creep twenty feet. I was beginning to gain confidence, when a gust of wind puffed me toward the mast. I flung out an arm and found nothing but air. My legs buckled; my arms waved.

My feet slipped.

Thirty feet aloft, one hand was all that kept my head from splattering on the deck like a rotten melon. The newly healed skin on my arms stretched painfully. Sweat loosened my grip; the wind caught me by the waist and hurled me over the sea.

"Easy does it!" called Bram.

I glanced down. Some soldiers were holding a funeral. I saw them push two canvas-wrapped bodies over the rail. At the same time, a growing crowd of sailors watched me struggle, and, if I knew them at all, wagered bets on my fate. Heartless!

Wager all you like. I've done this a hundred times before. Two hundred times.

I swung my free arm up and grabbed the rigging. Now for my feet. I willed myself to stop struggling, to float with the wind instead of against it. Kicked out and missed, my bare foot scraping rough cord. Kicked again and this time found rope. Safe for the moment, I took in deep breaths of sea air.

This is, perhaps, somewhat more difficult than climbing in my gymnasium.

"Nicely done!" Bram shouted down to me. "You're nearly there. Now listen carefully. This next part's tricky!"

"Excellent," I muttered. "I was just thinking things were getting rather dull."

"You see that hole?" I looked where he pointed. The mast and rigging went through a hole in the center of the wood platform. "It's called the lubber's hole," Bram called.

Good enough. I can make it to the lubber's hole.

"Real seamen *never* use the lubber's hole. We go round and over the top of the platform like this."

More rigging stretched away from the mast up to the outside edge of the platform. Bram scuttled up this rigging like a beetle, back to the sea, face to the sky.

I don't want to be a real seaman! I want to be a lubber! I longed to shout. But it wasn't true. I wanted to be a real seaman very much.

"Now your turn!" he encouraged me with an overbright smile.

I knew if I hesitated I might never move at all. I swung out an arm . . .

"Steady now!" he called.

. . . grabbed on . . .

"Mind the topsail," Bram advised. "It'll give you a good bonk on the head."

. . . and jumped, wrapping my legs around the line like Bram had so I was leaning backward over the ocean.

"That's it! You got it now!"

Inching, straining, eyes tearing in the vile, despicable, loathsome sun . . .

"Here!" Bram leaned over the railing, just above me. He grabbed hold of my wrist and yanked. I landed on my belly on the slatted wood.

I will not kiss the planks.

"Have a rest and we'll head up some more."

"Can't we talk here?" I asked.

Bram shook his head. "Too close. We need to go all the way up for this."

I sat up. "Then save the rest. I don't need it."

"Good man," Bram said.

The climb to the next platform was faster, although the higher I went, the more I felt the pitch and roll of the ship. Pride swelled in my chest when I went over the rail unaided.

"Lucky for us there's no weather today, hey?" Bram said.

Lucky indeed. I leaned on the rail and felt the fear trickle from my liver. I'd done it at last! I'd climbed to the top of the mast like a regular sailor. I was stronger than Atlas! I—

Bram clapped me on the shoulder. "Just one last bit and you're there."

I beg your pardon?

I squinted up the mast. A single rope stretched from here to the yard at the top. I'd have to wrap my legs around the lone vertical line and shimmy up. My hands already had blisters and my legs were trembling.

A hundred times before. Two hundred times—

I took hold and jumped. Stretched thus, my body swayed like laundry on a line. I twisted my legs around the rope and pulled.

Blisters burst, ankle bloody. The sails snapped in the wind, and I clung tighter. My cap slipped from my head, bounced off a sail, and rode the currents to the outstretched hand of a sailor on the deck below. I saw him wave his prize in the air while his mates cheered.

You'll give that hat back or I'll make you, you cheeky bandit.

The yard was within reach. I grabbed the solid wood and hoisted myself up. Bram climbed next to me and we two perched on either side of the mast, much narrower at the top, with an arm holding on. We sat on the yard with our feet dangling in the air, gazing a dozen miles out to sea.

"Well?" Bram asked.

"Better than helping Barometer Piet with the chamber pot," I said.

But in truth, now that we'd reached the top of the world, I would have gladly risked my life ten times over to come again. Far below us, the men crowded the deck like a good catch of herring released from a net. White foam dotted the green sea, and every so often the sleek curve of a dolphin's back crested the waves. Up in the sky, pearl mist swathed the sun. There was only the sound of the wind, nothing but clean air to breathe. I never wanted to leave.

"It's my favorite place too," Bram said.

Together we watched the glittering sea in silence. It

seemed the whole world was nothing but water, the *Lion* its only earthbound creature.

"May I ask you a question?" I said.

"It's been since yesterday. I was wondering when you'd start again."

I ignored his impertinence.

"Where are we?"

"In the Atlantic, maybe six hundred sea miles east of Brazil," he said. "We sailed southwest from Holland around the doldrums and then shifted southeast at Trindade Island to chase the trade winds. Pretty soon we'll head due south. There'll be a lot more weather down there, and those big winds in the forties'll blow us clear to Cape Town."

My mouth hung open like a simpleton's. "However do you know all that?"

"The captain lets me sit in sometimes when he teaches the midshipmen their astronomy and navigation. And the quartermaster don't mind me asking questions. Even the pilot'll name a star or two if I can get him to sit still long enough."

I leaned against the mast and tilted my face to the sun, now warm, nourishing, forgiven.

"Miss Petra?"

"Hmm."

"I need to tell you something."

I heard the seriousness in his voice and understood that

Bram hadn't brought us to the top of the mast simply to enjoy the view. It was also one of the only private places on the ship.

"There's mutiny afoot," he said, voicing the dirtiest word on any vessel.

"A mutiny! Who? *Why?*"

"They're aiming to bite the VOC payroll," he said. "I don't know every cove who's in on it or how they mean to do it or when. Just that there's a plan."

Bram had no need to tell me that mutiny usually ended in death—either the captain's and the men loyal to him or the failed mutineers'—Albertina used to read aloud the stories of the trials in the broadsheet newspapers.

"Does Paulus know?" I asked.

He told me of his conversation with his father. "But he won't say more. If we can figure out who's in and what they're planning, we can decide which side we want to be on."

"You'd side with the mutineers?"

"I might! And you should think on it too, *Miss* Petra De Winter. You can't be a boy forever. And then what? You got two choices and you know it. You find a cove to marry or you go work yourself to death. But if you had enough money, you wouldn't have to do either."

"You don't know that! I've years to figure out another way. And, besides, stealing is *wrong*. And so is mutiny. It's the worst kind of treachery."

"Is it stealing when every coin in those chests was earned on the backs of ordinary men? You know what's *wrong*? Wrong's when your only choice is being a slave on land or working like a slave on a boat you can't ever leave. That letter from De Ridder's my only chance at a free life, and even if he writes it, the fancy nabobs in Amsterdam still might turn me away. Seems to me it's the rich coves who decide what's the *worst kind of treachery* and they do it so's the poor coves work harder and harder to make the nabobs richer and richer."

"Do you really believe that?"

"I think I might."

I could well understand Bram's feelings and how an otherwise good-hearted sailor might be willing to consider mutiny for three million florins. My father was one of those rich nabobs, after all. But what about honor? What about loyalty? Stealing was stealing, and De Ridder seemed to be a decent man.

Bram interrupted my thoughts. "Look, I'm not saying we should do anything. I'm just saying we should find out as much as we can so we can decide what's best."

I stared down at the swirling sailors again. Any one of them could be part of the plot. How far did it spread? I thought of the men I'd come to know so far: Clockert, Lobo, Jaya, Louis, the Polish trio, the twins Gos and Goth, Barometer Piet.

Barometer Piet.

His conversation with Jaya took on fresh meaning. I pictured the crinkles around his eyes and remembered the strength of his mangled grip when he took my hand. His gratitude to me for saving his life. Could my friend be plotting to overthrow the captain and steal three million florins from the Dutch East India Company? I wrestled with an urge to protect Barometer Piet, as Piet was protecting me by keeping his suspicions about my identity a secret from the rest of the ship. But Bram had also protected me—at great risk to himself.

"I may have overheard something," I said. "Perchance it's nothing . . ."

"Tell me anyway."

"Jaya came to see Barometer Piet in the infirmary. He said Commander Van Assendorp wanted to know how Piet fared and when he would be healed. Barometer Piet got angry and told Jaya to tell Van Assendorp—well, I won't repeat exactly what he told Jaya to tell Van Assendorp because it was rude, but Piet did say, 'If anything goes amiss, it'll be the wind and the weather, not Barometer Piet.'"

Bram considered what I told him and said, "Aye, sounds like Piet's in on it. I already knew about Jaya. Kosnik the smith too—hey! Hold fast a minute . . ."

Bram jumped onto the yard, hanging on to the mast with one hand and scanning the sea behind us. His black pigtail whipped about in the freshening wind.

"You see that, Miss Petra?" he said, suddenly full of excitement. I peered in the same direction but saw nothing. "Aye, I think it is. It's . . . *Sail ho!*" He smiled down at me. "I've always wanted to do that."

"What do you make out, Mister Broen?" shouted Van Plaes from the deck.

"Can't say for sure, sir," Bram called.

"One of ours?" yelled Van Plaes.

"Too soon to tell!" Bram yelled back.

"What's happening?" I asked.

He sat down next to me. "It's like this. If the other ship's friendly—say Dutch or a stray whaler or even an English boat, since Dutch and English isn't currently at war—we'll pass each other and maybe stop to parley. But if the other ship's a pirate—and she could be; there's buccaneers in these waters—well, the *Lion*'s full up with cargo and VOC treasure, so she's low and slow."

"An easy target," I said.

"Aye. So if De Ridder knows what's good for him, he'll throw his pride into the winds and run."

29

Bram

The ship was gaining fast. Me and Petra and most of the crew was leaning over the rail trying to make out the colors of her flags or the shape of her hull—some sign that would tell us who she was and what we'd do.

De Ridder and Van Plaes was up on the poop deck with the goats and chickens, their spyglasses fixed on the spot in the water. Men near 'em relayed their parley to the rest of us.

"Van Plaes says she's got Dutch colors."

"Dutch colors."

"Captain says it could be a ruse."

"A ruse."

"Captain says it's a ruse."

Oak stood by his master, ever dignified. Every man of us was clammed up, waiting.

"Mister Grof!" De Ridder finally called to the bosun, who was peering over the quarterdeck rail.

"Captain?"

"She's no Dutchman. She's a buccaneer. Let fall the topgallants, if you please, which should favor us with a bit more speed. We must not be taken, do you understand?"

"Aye, sir," called the bosun. He called the orders and the crew raced to obey.

"Time favors us," the captain said to Van Plaes. "'Twill be night in another hour and I shall head south. With any luck, the pirate will not anticipate my change in direction and by morning we shall be clear of her."

"The sea will be heavier farther down, sir," Van Plaes said, his eyes like black pits over his sunken cheeks.

"With this cargo I am prepared to risk heavy seas, but not"—De Ridder looked into the spyglass again—"a thirty-gun pirate ship."

Just in case his plan didn't work, the captain ordered all hands—even the soldiers—to get battle-ready. Six hundred feet pounded the decks. If mine was maybe a little slower than the others, I figured no one would notice in the hubbub. Right away the soldiers got to tying pikes to the masts so's they'd be in easy reach if we got boarded. I couldn't think of much worse than having to stick one of those spears into some pirate cove's gut—

unless 'twas having him stick one into mine.

I headed below to the gunroom, passing the galley where Happy Jan and his mate cooked up the last hot meal we'd eat for hours—or maybe forever. Tixfor and the other lads hurried by me to the officers' cabins so's they could pack up all the fancy glass and lash the furniture down tight. In battle, breaking bodies was fine, but breaking crystal wasn't.

In the gunroom, Lobo and his team was making grenades out of rags and lead bars.

"Cheval could use your help, Bram," Lobo said, pointing at Louis next to a rack of shelves stocked with cans of gunpowder. "Open all the cans and make sure they're dry. Then prime the guns."

"Aye, Lobo."

'Twas good those cans had no sharp edges. My hands was shaking so bad I could hardly uncork the stoppers.

Petra

In the infirmary, Barometer Piet and I tore linen into bandages.

"Tell me what he said again, sonny. Every word. And make sure you don't leave nothing out."

I repeated the captain's conversation with Van Plaes. For the third time.

"Ach!" Barometer Piet groaned, thrashing his head

back and forth on his cot. He raised himself on his elbows and pointed a thumb at me. "It ain't right, those buccaneers veering so far offshore. Spanish silver ain't enough, so they got to come after us?"

"But surely we've nothing to worry about," I said, "seeing as how the *Lion* is so much bigger than the pirate ship and we've got many more guns."

Barometer Piet gave me a pitying look. "You're a greenhead, Albert, so let me lay it out for you. We're bigger, aye, and we got more guns. But them pirates is faster—a lot faster—and our big cannons won't be doing us no good when the picaroons steal the weather gauge and sneak close enough to board us. And while I'd stake my life on the sword arm of any able seaman on this ship, the riffraff on the soldier deck ain't good for more than target practice, and, between you and me, even some of the ordinary seamen ain't much good either."

"The buccaneers are skilled hand-fighters?"

"None better. But they ain't pretty about it, see? They start by slicing off the little bits—noses and ears and such. If that don't bring order, they'll go for hands and feet. I heard of a pirate crew that decided to make a show of what happens to resisters. They took two coves and stuck 'em through bottom to mouth with a sharp stick, then roasted 'em over a fire like pigs on a spit."

Surely Piet's talk was just tall tales. "And is that, um, *usual?*"

"Roasting men alive? No, I just heard of the one time. But ears and noses, aye, that's usual."

No grin tugged at the corner of Piet's mouth. He meant what he said. The pirates were as thirsty for blood as they were for money. I shivered in the cold damp and cast my eyes around the surgeon's cabin. In a matter of minutes, the *Lion,* which was to carry me to a distant shore and keep me dry and fed, could carry me to the bottom of the sea.

"Barometer Piet, it's exceedingly important that we outrun this pirate ship."

"Aye, sonny. *Exceedingly.*"

After supper had been doled out and preparations for battle completed, hands were piped to quarters to take what sleep they could before sunrise. I was checking on Piet one last time when the ship tacked southward.

"And away we go," he muttered, "with our tail between our legs. I tell you, sonny, I ain't exactly keen to take on a ship of pirates, but there's something downright shameful about running away from a fight."

What if it was a fight you couldn't win? A fight where your opponent—be it a single man or a ship of pirates—had murder on his mind and was faster and stronger than you? Nay, to my mind there was nothing shameful about running away from this fight—or others like it. The only shame would be not running fast enough.

The motion of the ship changed now that we'd shifted course. The boat tilted sharply and lurched with each choppy wave. Clockert's instruments clattered from the worktable to the floor and I ran to stow them in his trunk. The surgeon himself didn't even bother to look up from his journal.

"Good night, master," I said. He grunted in response.

I staggered to the curtain to the sick bay and braced myself against the wall. "Until the morrow, Piet."

"Get ready, sonny," he said, flexing his remaining fingers. "There's a storm coming."

30

Bram

'Twas the dark time before dawn and a steady rain beat the decks. Pa'd already stowed his hammock and was tying on his belt. So was Petra, only instead of hammers and nails, her belt was strung with medicinal stuff—needles, thread, bandages, small scissors and the like. Plus she had her short knife on her hip.

"You think we gave the pirates the slip?" I asked.

"Too soon to tell," Pa said.

We three headed to the fo'c'sle and waited for dawn with the rest of the crew. The muggy wind was steady as the rain, and a tarred jacket and breeches didn't keep the water from running down my neck and soaking my woolens. But 'twasn't the weather that was giving me the shakes. If the pirates had followed us south, 'twould be my first battle.

Up on the quarterdeck, the captain and Oak was grave as us crew. We squinted into the gray light, watched it smear the horizon and spread up. Soon we could see more of the *Lion* and, minutes later, the pirate ship.

Hounds of hell.

She was heaved to a quarter mile leeward, stripped of all but her fighting sails, black flag waving from the maintop and black pennants flying from her yardarms. She looked to be a fourth-rate three-master, but was fitted out like no ship I'd seen before. She was painted black all over—sides, rails, even her yards and masts. In the dim light, she might've been a shadow, 'cept for the gleam of muzzles crowding her sides like a mouth of iron teeth. Stranger still, they'd made her flush. She'd no quarterdeck or fo'c'sle, just one flat main deck from bow to stern. And no wonder: Flat's better for fighting. The pirates would have no trouble moving round and about all those cannons that lined the deck.

Soon as she saw us, she dropped sail.

"Duivel," the captain swore. "All hands to stations!"

"All hands to stations!" shouted the bosun.

Louis's drum popped like firecrackers, and the crew took up the cry: "To stations!"

All my hairs pricked up. The pirates only wanted the *Lion* and her cargo—they'd waste no time tossing her men overboard. Me, I just wanted to keep my skin.

The Lions was all worked up.

"Let's sink those lousy curs!"

"Hack and hew 'em!"

"Bunch a yellow shag bags, that's what they are!"

"Lousy cacafuegos!"

I swallowed hard and looked at Petra. It'd be her first battle too. "You'll do fine," I said.

"It's not me I'm worried about. I won't be anywhere near the fighting."

Me, on the other hand, I'd be in the thick of it. "Right, well, see you after."

She looked like she wanted to say something more, but I wasn't sure I wanted to hear it. I turned to go to my station, but Pa pulled me back.

"Stay close to me, Brammetje." Pa would captain one of the cannons and I'd be a powder monkey, running in fresh gunpowder. "Look to me. To me or Jaya and no one else, you understand?"

"Yes, Papa."

He searched my face. "It's good you're afraid. Makes you smarter."

Petra

In the sick bay, Clockert was spreading sawdust on the floor. He held out the bucket.

"Lay it thick. We'll need it."

I choked on the breakfast that rose in my throat.

"That you, Albert?" Barometer Piet called from the sick bay.

"It's me," I croaked.

"Oh, how I wish I could get out of this blasted bed. Doc Clock! Let me up, will you? What good am I down here, hey?"

Now that the fight was upon us, Piet was eager to join it.

"Mister Pietersen," said the surgeon, "you may consider leaving the bed when you can piss and dung out unassisted."

I finished spreading the sawdust and went to sit by Barometer Piet. "Have you ever been in a battle?"

"Loads of 'em," he said. "But I imagine you ain't, so here's how it'll go. We two ships'll get real close, close enough to see the sweat of fear on the other man's face. We line up, broadside to broadside, and let loose the great guns. I tell you there ain't no sound more beautiful than the blast of them cannons and no smell finer than fresh gunpowder. De Ridder will aim high, so's to wreck the pirate's sails and rigging so she can't steer. Then once she's crippled, he'll blast her hull. If she's smart, she'll surrender before we sink her."

"But what if the pirate wrecks our rigging and sails first?" I asked.

"Ain't gonna happen. It's true, she's faster and lighter. But we're Dutch." He grinned. "We got God on our side, don't you know?"

Bram

The *Lion* groaned. She didn't much care for going top speed under full sail in rough water. I squatted next to a twenty-four-pounder, rubbing my frozen hands. Not a whiff of air broke the stink of sweat and burning match cord. 'Twas just light enough to see the crews crowded around their guns, waiting for the call to fire. I wanted to get on with it already. I'd also be happy to wait forever.

The pirate was closer now. I could see her through the porthole over the barrel of the gun. She turned and her name stood out red on her black transom. I couldn't read the letters, but I knew the picture of the three-headed sea devil on her flag: *Lusca*. I'd heard tell of 'em. Arms like an octopus, teeth like a shark, bigger than a whale. They could eat a man in one swallow if they wanted, but they liked to chew 'em first.

Jaya hawked betel juice into a spitkid. Lobo whistled a shanty. I jiggled some nails in my pocket.

"Quiet!" shouted Johann Majoor, his voice cracking. I didn't envy him his job, commanding five teams of men, all older and more battle scarred than himself. But his lucky birth made him an officer, be he fifteen years or fifty.

Jaya squinted through a porthole. "Two hundred yards . . . one hundred fifty . . ."

Oh Lordy, here she comes.

"Ready about!" shouted De Ridder from the quarter-deck above us. The *Lion* made a hard turn windward to show her broadside to the enemy.

"Gunners!" yelled Majoor.

Pa poured powder into the touchhole and picked up a match. We could hear Louis Cheval up in the waist, those skinny arms beating the drum with all his might. My own heart was near as loud.

"Aim high, gentlemen," Majoor directed.

The gunners planted their feet.

"Fire!" shouted De Ridder.

"Fire!" shrieked Majoor.

The gun captains brought matches to the touchholes. A hiss filled the cabin.

Iron balls exploded out the muzzles of the cannons. The recoil was so strong the gun next to me snapped off its ropes. Four thousand pounds hit the wall, crushing O'Brian's arm. I wiped his blood off my cheek.

The men cheered for joy of landing the first shot. Pa whipped around and let out a long breath when he saw me still standing.

"Man down!" shouted Lobo.

A couple of mates carried O'Brian down to Petra and Clockert while swabbers stuffed wet rags down the barrels so's to cool the embers inside. Gunners poured in fresh powder and rammed wads of cloth in after. Two balls, more powder, and in under four minutes the crews was ready to fire again.

But the pirates hadn't been lazy. Before we Lions could get off another round, they let loose a volley of chain shot.

"Foregallant sail's down and most of the rigging!" shouted Tixfor, who was messenger to the gun decks.

"Fire!" screamed Majoor.

This time Dutch and pirate guns went off together. Two balls smashed the hull of the gun deck. A splinter took out the sword keep's eye—now he'd be half-sighted as well as tongueless. Another sliced Gos's forehead open. I gagged on the sour taste of other men's blood.

Petra

Clockert and I had our shirtsleeves rolled and instruments ready when the first of the wounded arrived. A soldier had fallen on a freshly fired cannon and seared his back.

"It's the *Lusca*," the solider cried, though I couldn't say whether his tears were from his burn or from fear of the pirates.

"Jochims," Clockert said grimly, sending the simple

case to me so that he could remain free to treat more serious injuries.

He didn't have to wait long. O'Brian arrived on the shoulders of his mates, screaming for his mother. Clockert assessed his arm.

"It'll have to come off," he said.

I looked up from my patient's blistered skin, which I was coating with honey and soap. "I'll be with you right away, sir."

From that point on, the wounded arrived in a steady flow. Burns, lacerations, broken bones. Shrieks, groans, pleas. One soldier tripped over his own feet and bit through his tongue. My heart clenched with each new body for fear it would be Bram's or Louis's, but beyond that I hadn't even a moment to take in the horror, which was a small mercy. We sewed and cut and wrapped, and when the wounds were too grievous, we did the best we could to make the men comfortable. Krause was there to carry the wounded in and the dead out, his face wet with tears and snot.

There was a crack and a crash, followed by a torrent of running footsteps. I looked up from a sailor's open belly. "There goes our topgallant mast!" Barometer Piet announced in his loudest hailing voice. A deafening roar of gunfire from the *Lusca*. "She's getting closer! Mark my words, she's making to board us—but not if we board her first!"

Bram

De Ridder sent me to take stock of the damage below decks. After checking with the shipwright in the hold, I went up to the quarterdeck to make my report.

"There's seven feet of water in the well but with the pumps fully manned, she's holding. Guns two and nine in the main gun deck is breeched, and eight and eleven in the upper. Five men dead and above a dozen wounded, sir." I ground my teeth together to keep from chattering.

The rain had stopped, and De Ridder looked over the *Lion* through smoke and mist. Sails flapped like beggars' rags and the deck shined crimson with blood. Van Assendorp shouted orders at the soldiers. A more desperate bunch had never seen battle—they held their muskets like farm hoes.

The two ships was almost hull to hull now. Maybe fifty Luscas was staring us down, and there'd be more below. With their wide trousers and scruffy beards, they looked much as we did. Only hungrier.

They'd board us any minute, and when they did, that'd be the end of us. Happy Jan shoved a sword in my hand.

"What do I do with it, Happy Jan?"

"Whatever you can."

The *Lusca*'s captain stood on his quarterdeck with a belt full of guns slung across his chest. Black hair grew down his forehead and a black beard grew up his cheeks to meet it. Through the space in the middle he eyed De Ridder, who eyed him right back. Each man asking himself about the other, *What will he do next?* The pirates was willing to die for their prize. You got to want something awful bad to take a chance like that. We Lions had no choice—'twas either fight or get slaughtered. With odds like that, you take any chance you got.

Petra

Louis Cheval sat on a table in front of me, chatting amiably while I sewed a shallow splinter wound in his shoulder.

"Ooh! Zat does smart, Al. Maybe just a little more brandy for the pain?"

"Any more brandy and you'll have a whole different sort of pain. Now hold still, Louis, I just want to do two more stitches."

Louis contemplated his fingernails while I finished my work. A violent explosion rocked the ship and I grabbed the table to steady myself. Clockert just missed stabbing a soldier through the heart instead of cutting off his arm. Our eyes met for a moment, and he let out a long, shaky breath.

"*Primum non nocere,*" he whispered. "The physician's oath. First do no harm."

"That's it!" shouted Barometer Piet. "Come on, mates, give 'em back as good as we got!"

As if in answer to Piet's request, a gigantic blast burst from our starboard side. "That's the way, boys!" Piet cheered.

Bram

Pa'd given over command of his gun to big Kosnik so's we could work with Jaya to patch the hull. The guns glowed red-hot. Most of the crew had stripped off their shirts and was covered in sweat and grime. Majoor had shouted himself hoarse and men was firing as fast as they could at any target they could reach. Giant sea swells sent a lot of the shots wild, some of 'em even missing the *Lusca* altogether.

Lobo and his team got off two shots to the other crew's one: swab, powder, wad, powder, *FIRE! Again!* Lobo's hair had come loose and black snakes whipped round his head. A fresh red burn scored his ribs, and both his hands was wrapped in canvas, but he drove his crew by pushing himself faster and harder than any of 'em.

Pa and me was swapping out a cracked beam when a recoiling gun took out a cove and three of his mates. I was staring at the mess of bodies—tangled arms and legs, crooked necks, blood and more blood—when a twenty-four-pounder smashed through our hull. Splinters sprayed the cabin. Then screams.

Lobo roared. He snatched the swab from his man's hand, reamed out his burning weapon, loaded, and aimed for the pirate gun that had taken down his brothers. Hit his target square on. Chunks of flaming iron spewed out of the *Lusca*'s belly. A bitter smell of burning flesh filled the air.

I froze with my hand out, still holding the hammer I'd been about to pass to Pa, trying to make sense of the pile in front of me. The screams faded away. Alls I could hear was my own heavy breathing.

How will Petra tidy 'em all up?

Another thought tried to come after that one, but I was stuck on the mess and the thought couldn't get through. How could such a thing happen? How would it ever get straight again? I tried to move closer, but the crowd was too much. I got pushed away. I pushed back—I had to get to Pa—but I was pinned to the wall. Through an empty porthole I could see smoke and fire chewing up the *Lusca* and spitting out her crew. When she cracked, bodies, trunks, hammocks, and ditty bags spilled out her broken halves. Lions lowered planks to the Luscas, but not one hand clapped on. The *Lusca* and all her crew was lost forever.

The floor pitched wildly and a bowl full of bloody rags flew off my table. I ignored it and finished stitching a wound on a sailor's cheek. "Next!" I called.

Before another man could shuffle over, two sailors burst into the cabin carrying an unconscious mate between them. "Clockert! We've a man down here. We need you right away, sir!"

Clockert didn't look up from a soldier whose scalp he

was refitting to his skull. "Jochims's table, if you please, gentlemen."

"Master, it's serious," one of them urged.

"Jochims's table," Clockert repeated. "I shall be with your friend momentarily."

The sailors laid the man on the table in front of me. In place of a bandage, his face was covered with someone's discarded shirt and what I could see of his hair was blackened with soot. But there was something awful and familiar about the color of the ginger strands on his bare chest. My stomach clenched. I looked down his body, his unnaturally still body, and my gaze stopped at the tool belt he wore around his waist.

My breath caught in my throat as I unwrapped the shirt from the man's face. First one side, then the other.

Paulus.

I placed a trembling hand on his chest. Nothing.

"Noooooo." An inhuman groan from the doorway.

Through my tears I saw Bram sink to his knees.

31

September 1663, Cape of Good Hope, Africa

Bram

The *Lion* dropped anchor in Table Bay, the only tall ship in the harbor. We was stopped for the first time in five months. The rocking made me sick.

I leaned on the bow rail, facing shore. Dung-brown houses made shadows on the wet sand that looked like piles of ash. Next to 'em, fat Dutch farmers and their skinny Malay slaves worked the vegetable fields: on their knees, stuffing seeds in the dirt. Row after row after row.

De Ridder gave orders to hoist the secret code flags that told the VOC commander onshore we was the *Lion* and not some enemy in disguise. The commander must've liked what he saw, 'cause he gave us a ten-gun salute. The Lions all whooped and cheered. 'Cept me.

'Twas the crew's first leave since Amsterdam and they was all worked up. Louis tugged on my sleeve. "Come with us ashore, *Monsieur* Bram. We will see real lions—not like this one 'ere," he said, pointing to the figurehead.

"No thanks, Louis," I said, even though this was Africa and I could get off the ship if I wanted to. I just didn't want to.

"You sure, Bram?" Lobo asked.

"Some other time."

A cold wind blew. I tugged my hat lower, pulled my jacket tight across my chest like I could use it to cover over the hole inside. It'd come when my ma died. I'd almost lost the feeling of it in the months after we left Amsterdam, but now 'twas twice as big as before.

Petra

I took my leave of Master Clockert in the sick bay. The injured men had either died or recovered in the weeks since the disastrous battle with the *Lusca*. Barometer Piet had gone back to a crew quarters with eighteen fewer men. The soldiers had lost twenty-four.

I'd tried—and failed—to rouse Bram from his misery over Paulus. I'd sat with him in our cabin—in silence when he didn't want to talk, which was most of the time. I'd brought him stories of the daily doings of the crew—who won and lost at dice, who passed a kidney stone, what became of the eye a soldier lost in the battle with the *Lusca* (sealed in a stone jar, preserved in gin).

I'd even performed a miracle of sorts and convinced Happy Jan to make Bram a cake. I waited to make my approach until after the rush of the midday meal when Happy Jan was at leisure on the fo'c'sle whittling some animal from a scrap of wood.

"Greetings, Happy Jan."

"What do you want, Jochims?" he said without looking up.

"Nothing for myself, sir. It's about my friend Bram Broen. Perhaps you've heard—"

"What do you want, Jochims?"

"Well, I've been trying to cheer him up a bit, and I thought, perhaps, something sweet to eat might—"

"You want I should make Bram Broen a cake."

"Oh no! Not you, Happy Jan, sir. I can do it myself, with your permission—"

Happy Jan bared his pointy teeth at me. "Nobody goes in my kitchen."

That evening I brought Bram Happy Jan's cake. The next morning, it was still untouched.

One sunny afternoon I found Bram drawing in the waist. Spread around him, anchored by pebbles, were charcoal sketches, black-and-white slashes of demons and dreariness. I left and returned a few minutes later with his box of paint powders.

"I thought you might like a bit of color."

Bram stared at the box and his eyes welled with tears. Then he collected his pictures and cast them into the sea.

But my failure with his paints gave me an idea. If he couldn't find joy in his artwork, perhaps I could find it for him. It took me several days, for I'd little spare time and no talent in this area, but when I found him looking out over the bow and presented him with my gift I felt some small pride.

"I have something for you," I said.

I handed him the first picture and he turned it one way and then the other.

"It's the moon," I said. "I'd nothing to use for color, but I thought it might cheer you to have a keepsake of natural, er, beauty."

"Oh," he said.

I handed him the next drawing.

"Stars?" he said.

"Precisely!" I gave him the last page. It was my best work.

Bram squinted at it.

"Can't you tell?" I asked.

He squinted some more. "Would this be a tree?"

"Yes!"

"And this?" he asked, pointing to the figure next to it

"A rabbit! Don't you see the long ears and the round tail?"

"I see 'em, sure, but what are those droopy things hanging off the front of it?"

"Those aren't 'droopy things.' Those are the front paws!"

The old Bram would have laughed with me over my pitiful efforts. This Bram just sighed and handed back the pages.

Bram had been in his hammock, face to the wall, when I went to say good-bye. He'd sat up just long enough to wave and mumble a few words of farewell. I could only hope that time would do for him what friendship could not.

I'd failed as well in my mission to make myself indispensable. De Ridder had thanked me for my service, which he said was commendable, and then kept his word and ordered me off the ship for good. But I was in no rush to see the place where I would leave behind everything left on earth that was familiar to me.

"I'm told that Pieter Van Meerhof is a competent surgeon. In any case, his competency is less relevant than his ability to room and board you," Clockert said, handing me an envelope. "Take this letter of introduction. In it I've given him a fair assessment of your skills."

"Thank you, master," I said.

I caught a ride with Gos and Goth, who were rowing to shore to exchange mail. They carried five months of crew's letters in huge tarred and leaded sacks, which they would leave onshore, under a rock etched with "Michael De Ridder, *Golden Lion,* Batavia." I listened with half an ear as they explained that the next Holland-bound VOC vessel to stop at the Cape would pick up *Lion*'s mail sacks and leave behind their own.

"See there, Al, that's the town," Gos said, pointing to a line of houses that fanned the shoreline. The wound on his forehead from the battle with the *Lusca* had healed, leaving behind a red scar like a sickle moon above one eyebrow. It made him look permanently surprised. "The town's only about ten years old, so it's mostly just a few houses so far."

"And a fort," Goth said.

"That's so," said his brother. "You got the town here and that's Table Mountain over there—the one with the flat top—and the smaller mountain just north of it—"

"Called Lion'th Head," interrupted Goth.

"And the long hill—"

"Lion'th Tail."

"Aye, Lion's Tail. And that's pretty much it. Not much to do here but the one alehouse."

The twins rowed in silence for a few minutes, which was fine with me.

"Mind you be careful to stay in town. There's a hedge fence around it to keep out the Hottentots."

"What's a Hottentot?" I asked.

"The black savages. They're called Hottentots 'cause of

the clickety clacks they use instead of words. Sounds like they're saying *Hottentot! Hottentot!*"

"*Hottentot! Hottentot!* Keep away from 'em. They'll eat you alive," warned Goth.

Hottentots were the least of my worries. My mind was full of Pieter Van Meerhof and whether he would hire me until another ship could take me farther east to the Asian lands or west to Brazil—anywhere but back to Holland. I couldn't think about parting from Bram and the other Lions when they left for Batavia in three weeks' time.

The beach was aswarm with Lions off-loading water barrels from a long wooden jetty, a bridge on beams that the men used to roll empty barrels from ship to shore. From there they would push the barrels to a freshwater brook for cleaning and refilling before loading them back on the ship. I'd miss out on the pleasure of drinking that new water.

I scooped up a handful of sand, cool and damp in the late winter sunshine, and let it spill through my fingers. After months at sea, I felt the solid ground moving beneath my feet and I fought to keep my balance.

A guard at the fortress gave me directions to Van Meerhof's house, one of several simple buildings that lined the shore with walls of unpainted wood under a thatched roof. I rapped on the door and smoothed my jacket and breeches while I waited. Oh, the filth! The clothes hadn't left my body in the five months since they'd replaced my dress and petticoats. To think that until then I'd never gone a day without fresh linen. My skin was brown from the sun but at least my face was clean—I'd scrubbed it with salt water—and my hair was neatly tied back. It'd grown long past my shoulders, but that was usual among sailors.

The door was opened by a plump native serving woman. She wore a Dutch dress and apron with a three-pointed cap to cover her hair. Her massive bottom stuck out behind her like a kitchen shelf.

"May I help you?" The woman spoke Dutch with a strange accent that sounded like she was swallowing her words.

"Good morning, miss. Albert Jochims here to see Master Van Meerhof."

"Are you ill?"

"No, miss." I explained that I'd been surgeon's assistant on the *Lion* and was looking for temporary employment. I took the envelope from my jacket and handed it to her. "I have a letter of introduction from Master Clockert, the ship's surgeon."

She narrowed her eyes, looking me up and down from her considerable height. "The doctor is not available." She began to close the door.

"Oh, but wait!" Pieter Van Meerhof was my only connection, my only prospect of work, of shelter. "Miss! Wait, please!"

The servant stopped.

"What?"

"Is the . . . is the lady of the house at home?"

Evidently, I'd chosen the worst possible thing to say. The woman's eyes and mouth twisted into little knots of rage.

"*I* am the lady of the house, you filthy swabber! I am Eva Van Meerhof."

A European surgeon married to a native woman? How was such a thing possible? But she sounded as if she was telling the truth. And she wore a gold wedding ring.

"I beg your pardon, *madame*. I only thought—"

"You thought a Hottentot lady couldn't be married to a white man. Well, you thought wrong. *I* am the first. *People are not always what they seem to be.*"

How was I to fix this disaster? I'd offended the wife of the man from whom I sought employment.

"Of course, *madame*, you are quite right. Please forgive me for my stupidity. And, if it's not too much to ask, would you be willing to give Master Van Meerhof my letter?"

Missus Van Meerhof examined the envelope. She tapped it slowly against her palm. I watched, appalled, as she committed a grave breach of manners and *opened* it. Read the letter. And tore it to pieces.

"My husband has no need of an assistant," Missus Van Meerhof said. "But I don't like the idea of you running around causing trouble. You will work for *me*. You will do what *I* tell you to do."

I weighed my options in a matter of moments. In a village this small, with more slaves than free people, I had none. "Yes, *madame*."

"Now go around back to the pump and wash yourself." She sniffed. "I won't have you bringing vermin into my clean house."

I found the pump and used my handkerchief to scrub my hands and face. Eva Van Meerhof appeared and dropped a pile of old but clean clothes on a bench. "Burn yours," she said, and left.

I stared at the bundle. I longed for clean clothes, and I had no choice but to put them on after being ordered to by Missus Van Meerhof. But how was I to undress without being seen? A wall enclosed the back of the house, so I had no fear of passersby, but if Missus Van Meerhof happened to look out her kitchen window . . .

Reasoning that a bottom was a bottom, I turned my back to the kitchen, removed my trousers, and pulled on the fresh pair. They hung over my feet and I rolled up the legs and pulled the string tie around the waist as tight as I could. Glancing over my shoulder, I saw no one in the kitchen. I pulled my blouse over my head—

"I knew it! I knew you was a girl the second I laid eyes on you!" Eva Van Meerhof smacked open the kitchen door and strode outside. "What game are you playing? Pretty young white girl thinks she can sneak in here and get cozy with the only free man not tied for life to the VOC?"

She'd known I was a girl before she saw the linen wrap I wore under my shirt. What had I done to give myself away? Was it simply that Eva Van Meerhof was looking for rivals, or had something about my person changed but gone unnoticed by the men I saw every day? Without a mirror, I couldn't know. My own self had grown unfamiliar to me.

With my arms still in the sleeves, I clutched my shirt to my chest even though my nakedness was covered by the linen bindings. "*No!* No, *madame,* I swear it! I admit I'm a girl, but that is a secret known only to myself and one friend and now to you. It's a disguise I wear so that I can find employment, not a husband. I have no designs upon Master Van Meerhof, I swear it. I'm only twelve years old!"

"At twelve I had already left my family and been working two years."

"Then we understand each other, *madame,* for I too have left my family. And I too need to work."

"Oh, you'll work, I promise you that. You will *work* and you will not *speak* to Master Van Meerhof. You will not *look* at Master Van Meerhof. And you'll go on being Albert Jochims or I'll have you *hanged* for *thievery.*"

32

Bram

We'd been in port maybe a week when I woke up itching from the inside out. The fog from when Pa died had burned off, and now I was like a hungry rat in an empty hold. I had to get off the ship.

I decided to visit Petra. I hadn't heard from her since she left, and now I felt bad about not even knowing if the surgeon had taken her on.

I found the Van Meerhof place easy enough. Finding Petra was another story.

"What do you want with Albert?" the native woman at the door wanted to know.

"Just to say good day."

"The boy is lazy enough. He doesn't need you to distract him."

"I wouldn't distract him, *mevrouw*, I'd only parley for a few minutes."

"Well, I am his employer's *wife*. I decide what he does with his minutes. And it's not *parleying* with you."

If Missus Van Meerhof thought I'd be surprised by a Dutch man marrying a native lady, she needed to look down her nose at me a little harder. There was plenty of such coupling up in the Indies. Some of 'em was married, though not my parents. The law said Pa would've had to stay in the Indies if he'd married Ma. He liked us, sure, but not enough to give up the sea.

I was a bastard. A by-blow. *Illegitimate.* And now with Pa dead, I always would be. 'Twas a funny thing about mixed-race Indies kids. Bastard or no, the girls were like princesses—all the Dutch men wanted to marry 'em. But nobody wanted anything to do with a mixed-race boy—unless he had a high-up VOC pa. The rules about staying away from Holland didn't apply to the gentry boys. They went to the fanciest schools in Europe, some of 'em. I was never going that route, and now I was back to where I started, 'cept I had no family along with no future.

"Please, *mevrouw*, could you at least tell me when Albert gets his half day off?"

The witch smiled at me. I bet she had Petra moiling night and day. "When I say so."

We'll see about that.

⌒

When I got back, Jaya pulled me up to the bow.

"How fare you, my brother?"

"All right."

He spit betel juice over the rail. "No, you do not—and that is natural." He sucked his red teeth with his tongue for a while, looking out at the harbor. "Your father was my friend. I miss him every day. But life goes on, as you know, and we go on with it." Jaya lowered his voice. "You remember when I found you with guns in hold?"

"Aye."

"And I say to you there are better ways to get money?"

"Aye, I remember, *Om*."

Jaya leaned over so he could whisper into my ear. "Some men and I will take back money the VOC stole from us. You will join us."

"You're gonna bite the VOC gold?" I pretended to be surprised.

"It is no less than we deserve!" Jaya said in a fierce whisper. "Who works heavy heavy and risks his life every day? Not Gentlemen Seventeen," he said, meaning the coves in charge of the VOC. "*Not* rich men in Batavia. And *not* captain of this ship."

"We do the worst of it and get the least," I said. 'Twas the sailor's lament. I'd heard it more often than "pass me the bottle." I'd sung the song myself.

"Now you understand me," Jaya said. "I promised Paulus I look after you if anything happen to him. This is how I look after you."

All of a sudden, I got mad at Pa for leaving me to deal with the mutineers, for leaving me with nowhere to go. Bleed and wound me for thinking one day I'd be free like other coves. Losing that hope hurt more than never having it.

I smoothed out my face. "I don't know, *Om*—"

"We have time, my brother. You do not have to decide now." He put an arm around my shoulders. "For now, only you look away while we borrow a few supplies, yes?"

And if I said no, I'd be surrounded by enemies, including my pa's friend. I nodded.

"Good boy." Jaya pulled a leaf from his pocket and added a pinch of betel nut. "Oh, and brother?"

"Aye?"

"You say nothing of this. If anyone hears—well, it will be very bad for you. You understand?"

Petra

Eva Van Meerhof made good on her promise of work. I rose before dawn to haul in fresh water and wood and to stoke the fire. I cooked breakfast, dinner, and the evening meal and cleaned up afterward but didn't serve. That job was given to Rachel, the old Hottentot maid, who used her new leisure hours to chew dagga, a local leaf that kept her giggling over nothing or taking long naps. When Rachel wasn't laughing or sleeping, she gossiped with Eva Van Meerhof in their strange language full of clicks and clacks.

I swept the packed-earth floor and dusted the collectibles in the oak cupboard in the sitting room. I beat the carpets that hung on the walls, washed the linens, pressed Missus Van Meerhof's clothing but not her husband's— she reserved that task for herself. In the evenings I knitted or sewed until I was blinded by tears of exhaustion, and then I battled nightmares for a few hours on a straw mattress in the kitchen next to snoring Rachel.

It was something like my old life but without the help and comfort of Albertina. And it was the life in store for me should I marry a man not wealthy enough for a servant.

By contrast, the life of a surgeon's assistant—or even an ordinary sailor—seemed luxurious. But in the week I'd been here, no ships of any size had entered the harbor and I didn't know when the next one was due. Sooner or later one would come, and I would try to join its crew. If that ship wouldn't take me, I'd try for the next. But what if I had to leave without saying good-bye to Bram? Perhaps he wouldn't notice. He'd made no effort to see me, after all.

A week into my stay, I still hadn't met Pieter Van Meerhof. He'd been away on some business, but I guessed he was the handsome man who'd just come into the kitchen. Van Meerhof wasn't tall, but what he lacked in stature, he made up in muscle, in good teeth, and good humor. No wonder his wife didn't relish the idea of a new young woman in town. Pieter Van Meerhof looked like a man with healthy appetites.

"You must be the boy Missus Van Meerhof has told me about!" He clapped me on the shoulder and I stumbled forward a few steps.

"Albert Jochims, master."

"And how are you finding your new position, Albert?"

Eva Van Meerhof came into the kitchen and glared at me over her husband's shoulder.

"Excellent, master."

Missus Van Meerhof swept around the table. "Good morning, my love! How fare you?" She snatched a piece of buttered toast from my hand and fed it to him.

"You came from the *Lion*?" Van Meerhof asked with a full mouth.

"Yes, master."

"What was your position there?"

"Surgeon's assistant, master."

I blurted it out before I could think of anything better. Missus Van Meerhof looked like she wanted to fillet me with a pair of kitchen shears and throw me to the pigs.

"Surgeon's assistant? Eva, why didn't you tell me?" He put an arm around his wife's broad shoulders. "I have need of your skills, boy. There's fever in town."

"Oh, no, sir," I said, too scared to look at Missus Van Meerhof. "I was only an assistant for a week or two. Before that I looked after the chickens. I don't know much of anything. I don't think—"

"Nonsense!" pronounced the surgeon. "I have no assistant at present, therefore you can only improve my situation. Eva, dear, you won't mind if I borrow Albert for a couple of weeks until this fever dies down?"

Missus Van Meerhof beamed at her husband, a model of loving kindness. "Of course not!"

"Come see me after breakfast, Albert," Van Meerhof said.

Missus Van Meerhof waited for him to leave the kitchen before grabbing me by my arms. She ground her thumbs into my shoulders and leaned down until we were nose to nose.

"Not. Very. Smart."

I clenched my teeth to keep from saying what I wanted: that she was a horrid, nasty, miserable woman.

"Are you giving me the eye?" she said.

"No, *madame.*"

"Don't lie to me. I know what I see in front of my face. You think you're *better* than me. Well, you think *again.* Just wait a few years when *every* eye that looks at you knows what you are—not just *sharp* eyes like mine. You wait and you see how much you need a man, and you wait and you see what you'll do to *keep* that man when it's either him or the *tobacco fields.* Him or the *tanner.* His nice house or the whorehouse. You wait and see what you'll do then. *Miss.*"

33

Bram

I knocked on De Ridder's door and stuck my head around when he answered.

"Beg your pardon, Captain," I said. "Is this a good time to fix up your lazarette?"

"My lazarette?" the captain said from his desk.

"Yes, sir," I said, moving aft to the storage locker on the far wall of the cabin. "Slippert said the latch was broke and needed fixing up." Slippert hadn't, but I'd seen it when I came for dinner.

"I confess I hadn't noticed, but that's why I have Slippert. The man never misses a thing."

More like the man misses most everything, including the latch he uses every day that's been broke for months.

I got down on my knees and started working on it. Oak sniffed around my toolbox. I scratched his ears a bit and he lay down for a rest.

I coughed.

The captain kept studying his charts.

I coughed again.

"You're not coming down with that fever, are you, Broen?"

"Me, sir?" I said through the hinge pins that I'd stuck in my mouth to keep handy. "Not at all. It's only some dust."

The latch was fixed but 'twouldn't do to finish too soon. I set to greasing the hinges.

"But it does seem like the fever is spreading," I said. "Seems like Clockert's got more cases every day."

"Indeed," the captain said, looking up from his charts. "It worries me deeply."

"Things keep going the way they are, Clockert's going to need an extra medical man to help him."

"Is that so, Broen? Did Clockert tell you that himself?"

"No, sir," I said, wiping my hands with a rag. "Just my own conjecturing. I bet Master Clockert is missing Albert Jochims. The sick bay isn't near so tight now he's gone." I finished packing my tools and stood. "Lazarette's working nice and smooth, Captain. Is there anything else I can do for you while I'm here?"

"No thank you, Broen. I believe you've accomplished all you set out to do."

Petra

My plight grew even worse after I became Van Meerhof's assistant. No matter how many hours I put in with the surgeon, his wife expected me to keep up with my domestic chores, and so I rose earlier and went to bed later than I had before. When I worked in the house, Eva Van Meerhof was always there, looking over my shoulder and finding fault. At night, during my few hours next to Rachel in the kitchen, I tossed on my straw pallet, imagining the farthest corners of the world. I'd still heard nothing from Bram. Loneliness and worry were my only companions.

Two weeks after joining the Van Meerhof household, Pieter Van Meerhof found me while I was on my knees brushing the inside of the kitchen hearth.

"There you are, Jochims! How would you like a walk in the countryside? We've so many fever cases now, my supply of wood sorrel grows low. You'll find plenty of it near the lake at the bottom of Table Mountain."

I sat back on my heels and pushed the hair off my face with the back of my hand. "As you wish, sir."

"Be careful the Hottentots don't skin you alive," Eva hissed in my ear as I walked out.

Being skinned alive might not be such a bad fate. At least I should be free of Eva Van Meerhof.

I walked through town with an empty sack slung over my shoulder, barely sparing a glance at the stout Dutch farmers, clay tobacco pipes dangling from the corners of their mouths, chatting in the road with red-faced VOC officials who sweated under stiff collars and heavy black cloaks. Some Lions were loading provisions into a small boat. I looked for Bram, but he wasn't among them. The *Lion* herself stood sentry at the mouth of the bay, fresh paintwork on her transom gleaming red, blue, and gold in the afternoon sun. I stared at the Dutch flag until my vision blurred.

"Stop being maudlin, Petra De Winter. You've no time for it, and it shall do you no good in any case."

A hedge of bitter almond surrounded the settlement to separate the Dutch from the natives. I passed through a gate and followed the path that Van Meerhof had described. Once the town was behind me, I was the only person within sight. Dry earth and low shrubbery gave way to scrubby trees and new spring grass. I passed a herd of grazing sheep and a Hottentot shepherd dozing in the shade of a tall tree. He wore an animal skin around his shoulders and a smaller hide around his hips. A leather pouch hung from his neck, and his arms were decorated with ivory bangles. The shepherd spit out a mouthful of dagga leaves and greeted me with a few clicks and clacks. I waved back.

"Dear me. I must be careful that Hottentot doesn't skin me alive."

The lake was small enough that a person who could swim could cross it easily. I wondered if it was shallow enough to wade through, but I wouldn't dare try. The brown water looked like it could hide any number of wild beasts. Bram had drawn me pictures of fantastical animals called crocs and hippos, creatures with mouths full of sharp teeth set in enormous jaws that opened wide enough to swallow a goat whole. I'd no wish to meet them in these waters. After all, I wasn't much bigger than a goat.

Finding the wood sorrel was simple, its white flowers easy to spot in grass that was just beginning to turn green in the new spring. I kneeled on the soft ground and began to fill my sack.

"Miss P—Albert! Albert Jochims!"

Bram! He came running from the path and pulled me up onto my feet. We stood for a moment, him panting, me gaping, neither of us quite knowing what to do next. There were shadows under Bram's eyes and his hair looked like he hadn't combed it since I'd left the *Lion*. But at least there was some life in his face where before there'd been none. Finally, we spoke at the same time.

"What—"

"How—"

"How—"

"What—"

"You first," he said.

"No, you."

Bram wiped his hands on his trousers. "That evil lady said you was here."

"Missus Van Meerhof?"

"Are there two of 'em?"

"No," I said, laughing now. "One's plenty, thank you very much. I'm surprised she told you where to find me."

That seemed to remind him why he'd come. "Miss Petra, we got to go!"

"Go where?" Out of the corner of my eye, I spied movement on the far side of the pond.

"Back to the *Lion*. Right now."

"But—*Bram*—"

"There's no time. The captain says—"

"*Bram*—"

"We only got—"

"Bram! *Look!*"

I grabbed his shoulders and turned him around.

He was silent for a moment and then: "*Zounds*. Elephants!"

"Are you sure that's what they are?" I whispered. "They're not hippos?"

"Oh, no, Miss Petra. These are elephants. I'm sure of it. See the long noses? They're called trunks."

A chain of them were making their way into the water, linked trunk-to-tail, ears flapping lazily. Two babies about the size of cows, and six grown ones, their steps slow and heavy. Once in, they used their trunks to stir the water and scoop it up to drink.

"We had 'em on Java," Bram whispered. "I knew a

farmer there who used one to plow his fields. He let me ride it once."

"How extraordinary! What did it feel like?"

"Hairy."

I elbowed him in the ribs. The elephants were spraying each other now, the little ones prancing around the grown ones' legs.

"Do you think they're all related?" I asked.

"Couldn't say. Two of the big ones must be mothers," he said, "but maybe the others is just part of the tribe."

A family by choice. Linked together, none could get lost or left behind.

Bram took my hand.

"Zounds," I said.

The elephants were on the move again, crossing the lake in our direction. Halfway across, the little ones had to swim, which they did with their trunks in the air and much prodding from their elders.

"We got to go, Miss Petra," Bram said, tugging gently on me. "Those elephants look tame enough, but they'll trample us if we get too close."

I dragged my eyes away from the herd and went with him back to the path. "What was the important thing you were trying to tell me?" I asked.

"Fever's spread through the ship," he said, the smile darkening on his face. "The captain says he needs you with us to Batavia, but you got to come now. We're being quarantined."

The captain needed me. I could go back to the *Lion* and my friends there, away from Eva Van Meerhof, daily drudgery, and sleepless nights. Perhaps I should have thought harder about the words *fever* and *quarantine,* but they seemed such tiny, insignificant things next to *ocean* and *East India.*

I looked down at the sack of wood sorrel in my hands. "We shall go straightaway. I've nothing to pack. Only I must leave this medicine for Master Van Meerhof."

We raced along the path and through the small town, the spring sun warm on our faces. Missus Van Meerhof was outside her house, sweeping her front steps.

"Here," I said, tossing her the wood sorrel. "I'm going back to sea."

The shock on her face was plain and quickly turned to indignation.

"In *my* clothes?" she said, pointing at the trousers and shirt she'd made me put on when I arrived.

"Why, yes," I laughed. "And thank you very much, *madame.*"

I took Bram's hand and we ran off before she could protest further.

"Do give my best regards to your husband, will you?" I called over my shoulder.

34

Bram

On our way back to the *Lion* I asked Petra how it was for her working for that lady.

"Put it this way," she said. "I prefer doctoring a crew of plague-ridden sailors to remaining in service with Missus Van Meerhof."

"I got that idea of her when I came to see you," I said.

"You came to see me?"

"She didn't tell you? It must've been about a week ago."

Petra looked cheerly at that. When we got to the *Lion*, I headed to the hold to help sort provisions, glad to have work. Lucky for us, we'd already loaded fresh supplies for the trip to the Indies before the quarantine started. Happy Jan growled orders for storing crates of green stuff and barrels of salted fish and seal meat. Antelope dried on hooks in the ceiling, and boxes of penguin eggs was stacked in a corner. Best of all, every water barrel was full and clean. We'd have at least a couple of weeks before it'd spoil and we'd have to beat out scum and worms again.

Over in the next cabin Van Assendorp was shouting at some soldiers to shift the VOC treasure chests, the white scar like war paint on his red face. I'd never seen him spare a kind word for those coves, but what can you expect from someone who worked a slave ship? 'Twas bad enough to almost make me feel sorry for the soldiers. Van Assendorp had his sword out and two armed men on either side of him to make sure nobody got brave. I snuck a look at the chests. It seemed like there was more of 'em. Petra'd know for sure. I'd ask her to check.

Petra

The sick bay had never been so full. Not even after the battle with the *Lusca*. We'd taken over a good portion of the crew's quarters, and the room was sweltering. The open portholes did little good. All those fevered bodies packed together generated more heat than Happy Jan's oven. Makeshift beds covered every inch of floor. Clockert's desk was the only flat surface and even that was buried under papers, basins, medicine bottles and, if I wasn't mistaken, a lancet or two.

Krause's large body was wedged between two sick men whom he was feeding simultaneously. A spoonful of thin gruel between one pair of trembling lips and then another. "In you go," he crooned. Perhaps he was even sober.

"Jochims," Clockert greeted me while he examined the undersides of a young sailor's eyelids. He wore a scarf over his head like a pirate to keep hair and sweat out of his eyes.

"Master," I said.

"Good of you to join us. Kindly make use of these," he said, handing me a basin and one of the lancets from his desk. "I want four ounces from every man."

"Yes, sir." I took the bowl and tucked the lancet into a pocket.

"I'm going to see the captain about granting us more space. When you finish the bloodletting, assist Krause with feeding the patients. Happy Jan has a diet pot ready in the galley."

One by one I opened a vein in the arm of a sick man and let out a moderate quantity of blood. I knew them all by face and some by name. The few who were awake and not delirious tried to summon a smile or some other show of bravery. I went from bedside to bedside, my heart like a stone in my chest, until I reached the last cot and the stone dropped to my gut.

"How are you, Louis?" I stroked his damp head.

"Al, you're back. I am so 'appy to see you."

And just like that I was home. I owed my life to Albertina, but this filthy, smelly place—and these dirty, sickly sailors—gave me more comfort than my father or his house ever did.

There was so little we could do for them! We could bleed their veins or purge their bellies. We could feed them and offer them barley water. We could sponge their faces and wipe their bodies. We could watch their suffering, but we couldn't ease it.

Clockert didn't return right away. "He hasn't left these rooms in two days," Krause said.

We looked helplessly at the sea of bodies.

"Mind if I take a rest?" he asked.

"Go ahead. Who knows when you'll have another chance?"

I sat at Clockert's desk, absentmindedly riffling the edges of a few papers.

"Do you know any songs?" Louis murmured.

"None you'd want to hear," I said. "I sing worse than a tomcat in springtime."

"A story then," he suggested.

I'd never been any good at making up stories. My mother had been gifted that way. She'd had a new tale of adventure every night.

But there was something I could do for the men. I picked up one of Clockert's books and began to read aloud:

"Let no man belong to another that can belong to himself—"

"Jochims! I've need of you." Clockert bustled into the cabin and began collecting supplies.

"Sir?"

"Come with me, please. Krause, stay awake while we're gone, will you?"

Krause snored in answer. I followed Clockert to a hatch amidships that I'd not used before. It led to the soldiers' deck.

"Prepare yourself, Jochims. Conditions here are not so nice as they are in my office."

It was good he'd warned me, but nothing could have prepared me for the sight and smell of the soldiers' cabin. We descended the few steps it took to reach the floor and surveyed the room from our knees, for the ceiling was so low even I couldn't stand upright. There was enough candlelight to see misery in every corner. With no room for cots or hammocks, the men lay directly on the hard deck, and between their bodies the floor was sticky from overflowing slop buckets. Unlike Clockert's infirmary, where the sick talked in low tones if they could or moaned if they couldn't, the soldiers' deck was silent but for the heavy, labored breathing of its men.

"Are they *all* sick?" I asked.

"If there's a healthy one here, I haven't found him."

One by one, Clockert and I visited each man. I cleaned

them as best I could and Clockert dosed them with whatever he had. The soldiers were mostly German and Clockert spoke to them in their language. But I didn't need to understand their words to know how low they were in body and spirit.

"Can't they be moved somewhere fresher?" I asked.

"I'm afraid not," Clockert said. "I asked the captain, but he said he hasn't space."

And so we shuffled on our knees from man to man, doing what we could while my rage burned along with their fever. No person should have to live in such conditions as these: crammed together, sun and space for only a few short minutes each day—and when the weather was foul, or the men were ill, not at all. These men were treated worse than prisoners. They were treated like slaves.

35

October 1663

Bram

When an ordinary cove died, his mates tied him up in sailcloth with some round shot for weight and a stitch through
his nose to keep him covered, offered up some friendly
words, and sent him over the rail, after which the sharks
took care of the burial. But when an officer died, or a gentry cove like cotton-faced VOC rep Isaack Van Swalme, the
captain called all hands on deck for a proper funeral.

The *Lion* was still anchored in Table Bay, too sick to
sail. Every week we got more sun and less rain. The day
was warm, the wind all but dead, and the ship reeked
of sick. Excepting Petra, Clockert, and Krause, every cove
who could stand was there in his best clothes. That is, if
he had best clothes.

I was wedged between Jaya and the Gos brothers in the waist, facing the captain and the reverend on the quarterdeck. Van Swalme's body lay on a table next to them covered in fancy linen.

"*Seigneur* Van Swalme's career began in Delft, from which place he exported cheese to Spain and France," De Ridder began.

What were the chances Van Swalme left some gelt for a funeral feast after the service? Or at least enough for an extra ration of penguin meat.

"He leaves behind his good wife, Bauwina, and his excellent children, Idesbald, Igor, Iks, Beeuwke, Balthildis, and one more who was presumably born this summer and whose name we've not yet learned . . ."

"We are better without him. Him and his fifty percent," Jaya said under his breath.

I broke free from my daydream about soft bread with new butter and got busy chewing my fingernails.

"And who's going to cover for us? Answer me that," Gos whispered back.

"Shhhh! Shut your gob," Goth said, looking around.

"We talk about it with others tonight," Jaya said.

Add Gos and Goth to the list of mutineers.

"Lord it be thy pleasure to bury this our friend in the bottom of the sea. His life is thine. Save him," finished the reverend.

"Save him," we said.

Three men slid Van Swalme into the ocean. His send-off may have been fancier than a common sailor's, but the sharks'd give him equal treatment in his final resting place.

"While he was fighting for his life, *Seigneur* Van Swalme remembered his shipmates. He asked that all Lions take part in a special meal served in his honor this evening," announced the captain. "Buffalo brought fresh from shore and double rations of gin are the menu tonight. That will be all for now, gentlemen. Return to your watches."

The crew whooped for joy. Maybe good food would blow off some of the black cloud that'd been pressing on us since the fever struck.

I headed below to tell Petra about Jaya and the Gos brothers but stopped just outside the sick bay. The smell was like a dog in the tropics three weeks dead and gone swampy. And 'twas hot as burnt brick.

Petra held a bowl for a sailor while he puked. Her hair was tied back in a scarf like Clockert's. Her face was paler than chalk with purple smudges under her eyes. The knobby bones in her wrists stuck out.

She looked over at me. "I don't even notice the stench anymore. Can you stand to come in for a bit? I just have to finish this."

I poked a toe into the cabin. The sword keep lay asleep or blacked out next to Tixfor. By the looks of him, Tix wouldn't outlast his master for long. I didn't like the cove, but I wasn't happy to see him die, either.

"Mister Broen, have you come for a room at the inn?" Clockert asked from his desk in the shadows.

"No, master, I'm here to see Albert on a personal matter."

"A personal matter, eh? Going for a swim on this lovely spring day? Or perhaps a stroll through town?"

Petra stowed the bowl and smoothed the blanket on the shivering sailor. "Master Clockert, may I have a few minutes' leave?"

Clockert waved her away. "'Gather ye rosebuds while ye may, Old time is still a-flying, And this same flower that smiles to-day, Tomorrow will be dying.'"

"Did he lose his mind?" I asked when we was out of earshot.

"It's how he amuses himself," Petra said. "Can we go to our spot on the foremast? I could use some air."

I thought she could use more than just some air—some gin and buffalo meat came to mind.

On the yard eighty feet up, Petra pulled off her scarf and the wind took her hair. Down below, I could make out De Ridder and Oak steady on the quarterdeck, while scores of other coves went about their work.

Petra was only half listening when I told her about Jaya and the Gos twins.

"They said they're meeting tonight. I was thinking I'd follow them," I said.

"Hmm."

"And another thing. The VOC trunks in the hold. Do you remember how many there was?"

"No." She scowled.

"You sure? 'Cause I'd cap downright there's more now than when you was hiding there. But how could they've taken on more trunks? Every man on board would've seen 'em loaded."

"Everything's been shifted. It looks like there are more because they're stacked differently. Look at that cloud," she said, pointing. "Does it remind you of a pair of shoes?"

"No, it don't," I said. "It reminds me of a pair of pistols, which is what the captain's going to be staring at before long. And us too, if we don't take care. I don't think it's the stacking, but I'd be sure of it if you could go down and check."

"Bram . . ."

"Miss Petra, it's important."

"Why?" Petra sighed. "What does any of it have to do with us?"

"We got to know who's who and what they got planned so we can know what's best for us. Right now we got two groups. There's the captain and the men that's with him, and there's the men who want the VOC trunks and'll have to mutiny to get 'em." She still had her eyes on the clouds, when what she needed to see was a ship with a couple hundred men and a few thousand pounds of gunpowder. "Whichever group wins, the other group's as good as dead."

"Why don't you ask Jaya about it?"

"If I do that, I'll have to tell him I'm in." I studied Petra's miserable face. Why such a fuss over a quick peek? "It'll only take a minute."

"I don't *have* a minute. Half the ship's down with fever, in case you haven't noticed. And . . ." Her voice cracked.

"And?"

She jumped up and grabbed the line, readying herself to slide down. "I *hate* those trunks!"

It made no sense. She made no sense. "But you'll do it?"

"Of course I'll do it," she said, her eyes tearing over. "You asked me, didn't you?"

36

Bram

Since Clockert'd taken over the carpenter's cabin, I was
bunking with Jaya and Lobo in the gunroom where all
the rifles and handguns was stowed. So 'twas no trouble
to keep a watch on Jaya and wait for him to leave for his
powwow. Right now, though, he was darning a sock while
Lobo carved Poseidon out of a piece of whalebone. I lay in
my hammock sketching a hairy orange ape stealing fruit
from a Javanese market. I'd painted such apes before—
they was common enough on Java—mixed vermilion with
a bit of umber to get just the right orange, then brushed it
on with a feather tip for fineness. But I didn't care much
for color and fineness now.

"Give us a song, Lobo," Jaya said.

Without looking up, Lobo started in on a shanty about a brave cove who dies and the good funeral his messmates give him. Lobo had the cleanest voice on the ship, no one could argue, and after a few verses I had that soft feeling that sad songs give you.

"Well done, brother," Jaya said when Lobo finished. He stood up. Jaya was small enough he didn't have to stoop and even had a couple inches to spare between him and the ceiling. "I must go now. I just remember something I promise to do for Van Plaes before morning. Do not wait up for me."

"We won't," Lobo said.

Did Lobo mean something extra by that? I couldn't stick around to find out. I shook off the gloom and waited half a minute before telling him I was going to the head.

Instead I took off after Jaya and just spied him going down the hatch to the hold. I lay on my belly and looked down. All clear.

And so was the hold, except for a couple of soldiers De Ridder'd ordered to guard the VOC chests while we was anchored in Table Bay. Which meant the meeting could only be in one place.

The hell.

On a ship the size of the *Lion*, crammed with hundreds of men, there was only two places with any privacy: the top of a mast or the bottom of the hull. The hell was a locker at the bottom of the bow. Spare parts and rope got stored there, and the bosun and his mate sometimes used it for a workshop if they had to. But anyplace was better than the hell. Cramped and airless, it heaved with every wave. Only the hardest stomachs could spend more than a few minutes in there.

I put my ear on the door. Voices.

I couldn't smoke who was talking over the smack of the water, so I rubbed some spit into the hinges and edged the door open a couple inches.

Jaya. Van Assendorp. Barometer Piet Pietersen. The Gos brothers. Plus a few others I couldn't see.

"I tell you we don't need him!" Jaya had his hand braced against a wall and was leaning over the twins, who was sitting on crates. "We will melt it and make new coins. No one will know it came from VOC and no one will look to us."

"He's right," Gos said. "Van Swalme just wanted his fifty percent. We don't need him."

"And uth to do all the work," his brother added, scratching at a raw saltwater boil on his arm.

"And risk our necks," said some cove I didn't know.

"It don't matter either way," Barometer Piet said. "Whether we need Van Swalme or not, we don't got him. So what do you say we talk about something else, hey?"

"We're gonna need a forge," Gos said.

"Kosnik can build one," Van Assendorp said, cracking his knuckles.

"The smith will be lucky to live to see another Sunday," said Jaya.

"How 'bout the gun maker?" asked a voice.

"Working on him," said another voice.

"What's the problem?" Van Assendorp asked.

"The sword keep."

So the Polish trio was split.

"Don't worry about the forge now," Van Assendorp said, ending the fight. "That much we can figure out when we get to the Indies."

"And the rest?" Barometer Piet asked.

"As planned," Van Assendorp said.

The men straightened their backs and made to leave. I eased the door shut and snuck back to the cabin.

Petra

Krause was snoring like a hog and even Clockert had collapsed over his desk. I longed to join them right there on the small, hard chair. Instead I hauled myself up and unlocked Clockert's storage closet—he'd long since allowed me, but not Krause, the key—and prepared to go count the payroll chests of the Dutch East India Company.

But when I opened the hatch, I heard voices directly below. It seemed that when the men had rebalanced the cargo, they moved the treasure chests directly under the sick bay, and there were soldiers on guard. I'd have to use the hatch near the galley.

I climbed down the ladder into the main hold unseen and slid around towers of cargo to the wall between the main hold and my old hiding place. I found the knothole and peered through.

There, stacked neatly against a wall, were the objects of every man's dreams. But I'd no need of such fantasies. I knew. Knew what it was like to avert my eyes from the glint of gold bricks stacked floor to ceiling. How it felt to run my fingertips over their sleek sides. The tickle of cool metal when I plunged my arms into a sack of coins, all the way up to my shoulders.

I knew because every coin and bar in those trunks came from the Amsterdam Bank of Exchange, the bank Father once directed, and there had been days, when I was much younger and Albertina was ill, that Father had taken me to work with him.

"Be quiet and stay out of the way," he would say. "I do not wish to see you until dinnertime."

And I had obeyed.

I doubted there was a soul alive who knew about the spaces inside the walls of the bank. Only a small child would hide under a table in a rarely used office, and in doing so would lean against a loose panel. Only a small child, with a child's curiosity, would push the panel aside and crawl into the darkness behind it, carefully replacing the board so that no one would notice it had been moved, but leaving it just a hair askew so that she could find her way out again.

The tunnels threaded behind every room in the bank. Including the vault, which was legendary throughout Europe for being absolutely impenetrable. Except by me.

Just the sight of the trunks made me sick.

I'd no need to count them. It was obvious there were more than before, all identical, guarded by two soldiers. I'd no idea how or why they'd multiplied, nor did I care. Bram had asked me to find out if there were more. I had, and there were.

I took far less care leaving the hold than I had entering it, so it took me a moment to figure out why a group of men would be coming out of the hell, and why they would fly into a rage when they saw me.

Gos grabbed my arm and slammed me against a wall. "What are you doing down here?"

"Lithening in at doorth, are you?" Goth said, leering at me.

"What? No! I was just coming from the hold." Gos's fingers dug into my flesh. "I needed—"

"What exactly did you need, eh?" Gos shook me hard.

The men inched closer, baring their teeth.

"Blankets!" I shrieked. "We need more blankets. Master Clockert sent me to look for some."

"He thent you, not Krauthe?" said Goth. "Don't thound likely—"

"Take a round turn, mates!" Barometer Piet pried his way through the mob. "The boy says he came down for blankets and I'll stand for him that he did. Any of you that's got a problem with Albert can take it up with me."

37

November 1663, Indian Ocean
Latitude: 39° S, Longitude: Unknown

Petra

I pressed a hand against my sore rib cage where there was a fresh bruise from a sailor who'd bumped me outside the galley. Barometer Piet's protection kept the mutineers from beating me outright, but in the few weeks since I'd been found near their meeting in the hell, I'd been tripped, jostled, spit on, and threatened.

The tide had finally turned on the fever—at last there were fewer men arriving at the sick bay than leaving each day, including Louis, who'd gone back to his own hammock weak but well. There were still some fever cases, but few enough to fit in one room. The toll had been heavy. Between the sickness and the battle with the *Lusca*, only forty-five soldiers remained out of an original hundred.

The sailors had fared better: their number stood at 151, down from 200.

The captain had given orders to sail for Java. We'd have to be lucky in wind and weather now that we were sailing during monsoon season, and De Ridder said he hated to depend on luck. Instead he drove the men hard, working them watch upon watch so that no one rested more than four hours at a time. Much as the men hated the work, they didn't hate their captain for it. Though they each had their own reasons, everyone wanted to get to Java. The *Lion* sped through the southern latitudes toward the very bottom of the world, wind and waves growing with every sea mile.

"Gentlemen, I do believe I see the floor of our humble office for the first time since September," Clockert remarked. "In fact, I'm certain of it. I know that very bloodstain. I made it myself."

I tilted my face up to the grate and relished the crisp breeze, but the fresh air did nothing for my head, which felt like the steel between the smith's hammer and anvil. I rubbed my burning eyes and tried to remember the last time I'd eaten a proper meal or slept for more than an hour or two.

"Krause, Jochims, would you please be so kind as to clear away the muck and lay down fresh sawdust and a sprinkling of vinegar. After all, it's spring here in the southern hemisphere. We're overdue for cleaning."

I moved for the broom in the corner of the cabin, but although my feet traveled in the right direction, the walls stretched farther and farther away. I reached, my fingers floating on air, long and skinny, like the legs of a squid. And now the floor tilted madly up toward me. I thought the ship must be cresting a wave, only we didn't come down the other side. The floor stayed vertical, close enough that I could rest my cheek on it, just so.

"Oh, my dear Jochims," Clockert murmured with no trace of his usual smirk. "Not you too."

Bram

The VOC trunks was disappearing. There was twelve when Petra went down there. Now there was ten. I checked every day. 'Twas easy enough to drum up an excuse to go to the hold. I'd say I needed some supply or another. The trunks was always guarded by a crew of two soldiers and I buddied up to 'em all. Nobody noticed me looking over their shoulder to count trunks while we chewed over the latest scuttlebutt. I knew which ones was sharp-eyed and which ones nodded off if given half a chance. I knew when they changed shifts and who they messed with. What I didn't know was where the trunks went and how they did it.

We was in the forties now. The roughest latitudes in the whole of the sea. Storms night and day, waves halfway up the mast. De Ridder had the crews working double shifts. 'Twas my time off, but unlike the coves in their hammocks around me, I couldn't sleep. So I sketched instead—though the ship was rocking so hard I could scarcely hold a pencil—and tried to work out the mutineers' plan. One thing for sure, nothing could happen while we was in these latitudes. Starting a battle on these wild waters would be suicide. 'Twas hard enough just trying to stand upright.

I wished I could talk it through with Petra. I drew her on her cot in the sick bay where she was now, using the side of the pencil to sink her eyes and cheeks. I remembered what she looked like the night I found her in Grof's locker. Still didn't know the particulars, but 'twas clear from her gold necklace and the fine cloth of her dress that she was highbred. Also, she'd been clean and well fed. Now, when she climbed the rigging in sailor's togs, no one would ever guess she was a girl. She even gulped her morning gin like a regular seaman.

Clockert'd stared down his nose when I asked him if Albert would live, and I took him to mean there was no sure answer.

I could do with a few sure answers.

My hammock kept knocking the bulkhead wall. With these seas, I hoped Clockert'd tied Petra to the bed and nailed her bed to the floor, else she'd die of a broken head before she died of fever.

I gave up sketching and headed out.

Hard rain blew across the deck, and gray light leaked from behind a cloud where the moon tried to shine. Ice hung from the bowsprit line. I turned up the collar of my jacket and tied my cap tighter. Lanterns bounced in the rigging, tossing yellow beams around. I looped a line around my waist and knotted it to the fo'c'sle rail so's I wouldn't get swept overboard.

De Ridder had lashed himself to the mainmast, and next to him Van Plaes was tied to the starboard rail. Together they commanded a miserable crew all tied on to whatever they could. Even in a fierce storm like this one—especially in a fierce storm like this one—there was crew in the rigging, all over the decks, and down below working the pumps.

"Here comes another one, Mister Grof!" shouted De Ridder, stretching a long arm over the rail with a lantern and scanning the sea.

"Aye, sir!" shouted the bosun, who was at the whipstaff in the steering room. There was no working the sails—most of 'em was tied back or taken off the yards altogether. Our lives depended on the steering of a cove who couldn't see the ocean.

"Now!" ordered the captain.

A huge wave loomed, but Grof steered the ship onto its top and made for flatter water.

"Look alive, Grof!" shouted a sailor somewhere up the mainmast.

A mountain of water sped toward us.

"Surf it! Surf it!" shouted the crew.

Grof rode this one too, but the next one rolled over us before anyone saw it coming.

A loose line lashed my face and I lost my grip on the rail. After that the water took me. Threw me down on the deck, tossed me up, and slammed me down again. And again. The line whipped around, but I clapped on to it and pulled myself back to the rail. Slumped down and clutched the posts with torn-up, freezing hands.

The ship leveled out, then heaved again, hard over, my side way up over the roaring sea. If I let go, I'd roll down the deck and crash into who knows what. My arms burned, but that was nothing compared to my raw hands rubbing on the bristles of a half-froze rope.

'Twould be so easy to slip the knot that tied me to this ship and let go. Let the sea take me. Find my place in the world at the bottom of the ocean, where there was nothing but sure answers. With her fever so high, Petra'd probably join me there soon enough.

Wave after wave hit the ship, forty feet from top to trough. Death was in those waves, and with each one I asked myself if it was mine. Grof fought 'em with the whipstaff; the crew fought 'em with prayers. Try as Grof might—and there was no one better than him at the helm—he couldn't ride 'em all.

"Holy Mary," swore a voice. I squinted into the dark

and saw a giant shadow getting bigger and coming at us.

"*Starboard!*" screamed the crew.

Too late. The foaming mouth swallowed the *Lion* like Jonah's whale, flooding her up to the quarterdeck. The water snatched my legs and hurled me against the mast. I reached for something to grab and got nothing. The *Lion* heeled sideways and I dangled like a fish on a pole.

If the line around my waist gave, or if I slipped the knot, that'd be it. Just one string tying me to life. One thin hope.

Turned out, one thin hope was enough. Now, when 'twould be so easy to let go, I didn't want to. Nay, I found I wanted to hang on as long as I could, if there was even a chance I'd make it through this storm alive.

"She's broached!" someone shouted.

The *Lion* was pushed to her limit. Another wave and we'd all be done for.

I gripped the rope harder, pulled harder, hand over hand straight up. My legs was swinging something awful in the wind, but I'd make it to the rail or die trying. Moving by inches, slipping as much as gaining, eyes and lungs burning with salt water, 'til the rail was there at my fingertips.

I clapped on.

Pulled one last time to wrap my arms around the posts and stayed there while the ship crashed down one mountain only to climb another. Forty feet up and down, I thought she'd flip for sure.

But she didn't. She found her balance.

I waited for the next big wave, but the worst of the storm was past. The *Lion* heaved but she wouldn't founder. I let go of the rail. Rolled to my knees, coughing up seawater. Men sprawled all over the decks, doing the same.

Van Plaes tossed his head and laughed.

"Is that all you got?" called O'Brian, shaking his one fist at the sea.

"Give us another!"

"Kiss my blind cheeks!" shouted Barometer Piet, slapping his bottom.

"You'll need more than that to take down the *Golden Lion*!"

"Mister Pietersen, go see the shipwright and ask him how the pumps are faring," called De Ridder. "A round of gin, men! What do you say?"

"Huzzah!"

With gin warming my belly and threat of death behind me, I felt like I could sleep, but not down below, crammed like cats in a sack. I needed air.

The ship's five small boats was tied up in the waist— stacked two, two, and one—and covered in sailcloth. They'd be dry enough inside, and I could count on being alone 'til morning. The paired-up boats was no good— chickens lived there in bad weather. I squatted next to the single boat and untied a corner of the tarp that covered it. The bottom was mostly dry. I climbed in.

'Twas warmer out of the wind. I stretched out on my back—and knocked my head on something hard. A big box. I scooted down and made a pillow of my hands. My fingers touched metal. I sat up and ran my hands over the box.

Which was no box at all but a trunk.

A trunk wrapped in iron.

I'd found one of the treasure chests of the Dutch East India Company.

38

Bram

"You wanted to see me, Master Clockert?"

Doc Clock sat at his desk and scrutinized me. The cabin looked like last night's gale winds had blasted through a porthole.

"I did. I'd like to speak to you about your particular friend, Albert."

"Is he all right, sir?" I looked over my shoulder, but the curtain was drawn.

"I treated him all night. To be honest"—Clockert cleaned under his fingernails with a scalpel—"I doubted seriously whether he'd live to see the sun rise. The fever was so high, you see. I purged him. I bled him a full eight ounces. I used the *speculum linguae* to administer oil of vitriol. And, finally, when those gentle measures had no effect on the poor boy, I determined I'd nothing to lose by administering an extreme treatment. Something I prescribe only in the most dire cases, as the cure can be as dangerous as the illness itself."

"What treatment was that, sir?" *Extreme treatment* had to mean the worst kind of torture. How could Petra survive it, wasted away as she was?

Clockert glared down at me. "I bathed him."

"In water?"

Medical coves all thought bathing in water was deadly, which was why no one ever took a bath and everybody stank. On Java we knew different. Still, Clockert must've thought Petra was at death's door if he put her in water.

And if he put her in water, he must've taken off her clothes . . .

"I did indeed. And it seems to have worked. The fever broke early this morning." Clockert waited for what he was telling me to sink in. Believe me, it'd sunk. "Now. Is there anything you would care to tell me about your friend—*Albert*?"

For two weeks I knew only heat and cold. One minute flames seared my vital organs, and the next ice laced my joints, crushed bone against bone. At times I was back in the hold, tearing my fingernails on the rough walls, fleeing the rats. Often I found myself in the front room in Amsterdam, the poker's orange tip bearing down on me.

Clockert drifted in and out of this madness like a mercurial ghost. He held me while I coughed and wiped phlegm from my chin. He caught the soup that I vomited in a basin. What my body failed to produce on its own, he wrested from it with lancets and enemas in an effort to balance the humors that had gone so badly awry.

After the fire and ice gave way, I slept. When I awoke, Clockert was at his desk, his pen scratching in a journal.

"You moved me," I croaked.

"It was more comfortable for me to witness your demise here from my desk than from that chair you are so fond of in the sick bay."

"I'm sorry to have disappointed you by surviving."

"You do not disappoint me, Jochims. You do, however, disoblige me."

"Master?"

"Surely I don't strike you as blind or stupid?" Clockert put down his pen. "I suspected you were female from the moment I met you—nay, even before that, for never has there been a human male with a knack for housekeeping such as yours. But a medical man notices things—a fineness of bone, a generosity of hip, a wish to keep clothes on after being keelhauled—and as a medical man, I can say, without excessive pride, that I am more skilled than most. Without *proof* of my suspicions, however, I could look the other way without fear of moral compromise. But now . . ."

Snippets of various medical treatments over the course of my illness flashed through my head. "Now you have proof," I finished for him.

"I do. And, since I attended you during your illness, if the captain were to discover your sex, he'd know that I'd been aware of your deception. I'm sorry, Jochims, but I'm only willing to risk so much of my personal and professional reputation protecting you."

"Does anyone else know?" I asked in a small voice.

"No one who hasn't known all along. Your friend Mister Broen was quite eager to confess all once I confronted him, but I assured him I had no interest in the details of your sordid tale. In any case, it takes no stretch of imagination to figure why a girl in any circumstance should choose to cast aside femininity in favor of manhood."

"And now?" I wished I could sit up instead of lie on my back like a beached codfish, but I was too weak.

"What happens next is not for me to decide. As soon as you're able, you must go and see the captain. I've already spoken to him."

It was over, then. My fate was in the captain's hands. "As you wish," I whispered.

"*As I wish.*" Clockert sighed. "I assure you that precious little in this life is as I wish."

39

Bram

I found out there was good parts and bad parts to being alone.

With Pa gone and Petra sick, I could go a whole day with nary a word from anyone. But being alone also meant no one bothered to hide anything from me. I was privy to private parleys and secret habits. I knew the sailor Joost Van Den Dool had a sweetheart waiting for him in Java—and a wife waiting for him in Lelystad. I knew Lobo was a Jew. I didn't know anything about Clockert, one of the only truly private men on board, but I knew, almost to a one, who was aiming to pinch the VOC payroll and how they was going to do it.

Trunks filled up with gold and silver was too heavy to move fast, so they'd have to be pre-loaded in the get-away boats. But if you pre-load the trunks, you need to leave something that looks like 'em in the hold so no one knows they're missing. That's why Jaya'd made doubles of the VOC trunks using wood from my stores and iron from Kosnik. When the dummy trunks was finished and loaded with clay bricks, Van Assendorp arranged for the Gos brothers to stand guard while other mutineers swapped out the real trunks for the fake ones. Now six trunks—with three million florins of gold, silver, and copper—was stowed in two of the small boats. When the *Lion* got to the East Indies, the mutineers would escape in the boats along with their booty.

But they couldn't sneak off without anyone seeing. Getting two boats over the side of a ship and down twenty or so feet to the water was a big affair. They'd have to fight their way off.

Jaya caught me the morning after my parley with Clockert when we was tying up our hammocks.

"One minute, my brother. I wish to talk to you," he said, looking over his shoulder. "It is almost time. You are with us?"

Was I? I still hadn't made up my mind, but here was Jaya needing an answer. I nodded.

"Smart boy. Your father would be proud of you." Jaya

filled me in on the details of the plan, most of which I'd already smoked for myself.

"But how will we get away? Won't the captain come after us?" I asked.

"Do not worry about Captain De Ridder. He will not be able to stop us after we flood guns with seawater and tangle rigging. We leave at nighttime and bar door to his cabin. His officers', also. No one will be hurt. I will let you know when it is the time—soon soon. All right?"

My pa wouldn't be proud. And 'twasn't likely no one was getting hurt. But I nodded.

"Aye, *Om*. All right."

Later that night Lobo and me played Sheep and Wolf in the waist on a board he made himself. He'd done a fair job of it too, with a six-point star in each corner. For once, his sheep was losing to my wolves. I had a pile of white pegs on my side, and Lobo didn't have either of my red ones.

I won the last sheep and Lobo grunted. The cove hated to lose. We switched sides and started another round.

"How's Albert?" Lobo asked.

"His fever's gone. Clockert says he should be up in a week or so." Petra'd have to see the captain as soon as she was fit, but for now she was safe in the sick bay.

He jerked his head for me to move closer and whispered in Portuguese, "Some of the men are aiming to steal the VOC payroll."

"I know," I answered in the same tongue. Like most Java folk, I could speak Portuguese and Dutch—and Malay, of course—at least well enough to get by, plus bits and pieces of what I heard on the ship. Picking up new lingo was never much trouble for me.

"You know?"

"I know who's in on it."

"Word is spreading, then," Lobo said.

"Who else knows?" I asked.

"The thieves themselves, of course. And I think only a few others. But more will learn of it soon, now that it's started."

We played a few more turns, me giving up a few more sheep but taking a wolf, before I said, "Tell me, Lobo. Why aren't you in on it?"

"Well, for one thing, no one asked me." Lobo flashed his white teeth. "And for another, I've no fight with the captain. He's been fair to me, never asking why the son of a Jewish gem trader would want to go to sea. He cares more about my aim with a gun than my religion. What of you, Bram? Are you in?"

That treasure was my best chance at a future, but mutiny didn't sit right with me. And then there was Petra. No one had asked her, either, but she'd never sign on if they did.

"Look, Braminho," Lobo said, "every man must decide for himself what he's going to do here. We don't know what these coves have planned, but I promise you this: It *will* come down to a fight. And when it does, you come to me."

"Aye, Lobo," I said. "I will."

40

Petra

I tucked a stray piece of hair behind my ear and straightened the cap I'd stolen from Louis Cheval all those months ago. I'd laundered my clothes in seawater and they chafed my skin, but at least they no longer stank. I'd cleaned my hands, face, and teeth and tied on my belt of medical supplies—my belly had shrunk a good inch during my illness. I wore shoes but no stockings. I didn't own any.

None of it mattered. Not what I wore or how I smelled. Or how tired I felt. What mattered was my sex and the lies I'd told to cover it up. What mattered was the captain. He could protect me or execute me, as he saw fit.

I crossed the quarterdeck, fighting the urge to flee to

the foulest corner of the hold. The day was warm and a light breeze filled the sails. But in spite of the easy weather and the promise of dry land and better food, I felt only dread.

Slippert showed me in to the captain's quarters.

"Albert Jochims, sir," he said with an elegant, if shaky, sweep of his arm.

"Thank you, Slippert," said De Ridder.

The great cabin was as I remembered it. There were the portraits and the crooked sampler on the wall and the ambergris on the desk. The captain stood at the window sipping tea from a delicate china cup with Oak by his side.

"Sit," De Ridder said.

Oak sat.

"You too," he said to me.

I followed his orders. The captain did not offer me tea.

"Who are you?"

"Petra De Winter, sir. Of Amsterdam." I folded my hands in my lap so De Ridder wouldn't see them tremble.

"De Winter? You're not a relation of—"

"Yes, sir. He's my father."

De Ridder slammed his cup onto the saucer. The fragile china shattered, splattering tea on the floor. *"Duivel!"*

Oak snorted and leaped to his feet. I whipped off my handkerchief and tried to blot up the spill.

"Leave it!" he commanded.

I went back to my chair. De Ridder squeezed the bridge of his nose until he regained his calm. "Miss De Winter, you have put me in a damnable position. The VOC forbids Dutch women from entering Batavia and yet duty demands that I bring you there until I can secure you safe passage back to Holland."

"But I can't go back to Holland!" I blurted out. "Please, sir, I'll go anywhere else, anywhere in the world."

"You shall return to Holland on the next available ship." De Ridder held up a hand to stop me from speaking. He lowered his voice to a near whisper. "And in the meantime, you shall do nothing to give away your true identity. Do I make myself plain? The men will not take kindly to you when they find out that a girl has played them for fools all these months. Lived in their cabins, nay, tended their sick bodies. You shall go on pretending to be Albert Jochims or it will go very poorly for you, indeed."

"Sir—"

"That will be all."

Lead feet carried me to the door, where old Slippert appeared to show me out. It may have been an accident when his elbow hit my spine and sent me sprawling, but I soon learned Slippert had wasted no time spreading the news. There was no mistaking the murderous faces of the men I passed on my way to the sick bay. And when Gos slammed me against a wall with his forearm lodged against my throat and whispered, "Only God can help you now, missy," I knew I had more immediate problems than avoiding the next ship back to Holland.

Alas, there are no secrets on a ship with two hundred men.

41

Petra

Clockert allowed me to bunk in the sick bay and I rarely left it. It'd taken all of an afternoon for the whole ship to know who and what I was. It turned out that being a lone girl on a ship of men was more perilous than being a one-legged chicken in a cockfight—especially when that unlucky girl has made fools of those men. The irony was that after all the months of pretending, I felt more boy than girl.

Bram insisted on bringing my meals after I returned from breakfast one morning with a swollen lip. When I tried to visit the head, Louis Cheval barred my way. "They're waiting for you there, *mademoiselle*," he whispered. Krause took up his duties as Clockert's first assistant again—a development none of us liked, but the men wouldn't accept the services of a girl. Once, they'd been more than happy to let me bleed them, delouse them, read to them, dose them, clean their soiled sheets and bodies. But none of that mattered now.

Revolting as it was, I missed the work. I missed the company, the easy laughter of mates who considered me one of them. And so I did my best to keep busy. I kept the workroom immaculate, every supply in order. I tried to read Clockert's books, but sleeplessness made the letters swim on the page, and so I spent many desperate hours inventing impossible schemes to avoid a return to Amsterdam.

With only a few weeks left before the captain expected us to reach the Indies, Van Plaes presented himself in the infirmary with a sore tooth. Clockert had stepped away and Krause was off duty. It was a rare moment with no sick men and no one in need of a shave. I was alone.

"May I help you, sir?"

"I'm here to see Clockert. Will he be back soon?"

Could this be an ambush? Was Van Plaes here to hurt me? But no, he was pressing his palm against his swollen cheek, in genuine pain and utterly uninterested in me.

"I believe so."

"I'll wait, then." Van Plaes sat down in Clockert's desk chair. He closed his eyes and leaned back, his head lolling over his lacy collar. "Can you give me something for the pain?"

His question took me by surprise. It was the first time anyone had asked me for help since my meeting with De Ridder.

"I'm sorry, sir. I think Master Clockert will want to look at you himself before prescribing treatment."

"I was afraid you'd say that," he slurred.

In the silence that followed, an idea began to take shape. Van Plaes was De Ridder's number one man. I didn't think I was imagining the captain's respect for him. What if I sent a warning to De Ridder through Van Plaes? If I helped the captain stave off a mutiny, would he allow me a favor in return?

As soon as the thought occurred to me, I felt ashamed. What lower form of life was there than an informer? But if the mutineers carried out their scheme, lives would be lost. As would my own, should I return to Holland. Perhaps there was a way to alert Van Plaes without informing on the mutineers outright.

"Do you not think, sir, that the ship has seemed out of sorts of late?"

Van Plaes groaned.

"It's almost as if the crew were preoccupied somehow."

Silence.

"Or at odds with each other."

Van Plaes swung his feet from Clockert's desk and sat up. "Whatever do you mean, Jochims?"

"Nothing, really." I kept my tone light. "Only that

it seems like there may be some kind of disagreement among the men, and perhaps"—I gave Van Plaes what I hoped was a knowing look—"the captain ought to be made aware of it."

In two swift steps, Van Plaes was out of his chair and inches from me. He was a tall man. He towered over me. "And *perhaps*," he said, "the captain *ought not to be bothered*." He grabbed my chin. "*Perhaps* little girls should be seen and not heard."

God's teeth, the first mate was a mutineer!

I backed away until I hit the wall, and Van Plaes stalked after me, black sunken eyes burning. This time he grabbed me by the throat. "You're a little rat, Miss De Winter— yes, I know who you are. And I know who sired you. You crawled onto this ship through some dark hole and hid yourself in corners, stealing our food, sticking your nose where it doesn't belong. And now the little rat is scurrying around going *squeak squeak squeak*. I'll show you what I do to pesky vermin who can't keep quiet." He tightened his grip. I clawed at his fingers, but he only grabbed harder, lifting me off the ground. My feet scrabbled against the wall. The light spilling through the porthole grew dim.

"Best not dirty your hands, Van Plaes."

Barometer Piet filled the doorway.

"This rat thinks I should tell the captain that the men are unhappy about something. What do you think, Piet?" Van Plaes spoke without turning around.

"I think you should leave the rat to me."

Van Plaes loosened his hold enough so that my feet touched the floor. I wheezed a trickle of air through my swollen windpipe. Barometer Piet gazed at Van Plaes with dead eyes.

"She knows too much," Van Plaes said. "Get rid of her. She'll talk."

"It won't do to have her go missing. We don't want the captain asking questions. But don't you worry. She won't talk. Not after I finish with her."

I looked for a sign that Piet was putting on a show for Van Plaes, but he didn't spare me a glance.

Van Plaes let go of my neck and straightened his immaculate clothes. Once again, he was first mate of the *Golden Lion*. "You're quite right, Mister Pietersen. This work is no business of mine. Kindly leave word for Master Clockert that I should like to see him in my cabin for a tooth extraction at his earliest convenience."

He strode out of the sick bay.

"Piet—" I rasped, but Barometer Piet held up his hand.

"I ain't gonna touch you, Albert."

I sagged with relief.

"Please, let me explain," I said, unable to raise my voice above a whisper.

Piet poured water from a jug into a pewter cup and offered it to me. I drank it in one gulp. It burned.

"It don't matter," he said, his soft gravelly voice sounding almost kind. Almost like his usual self. "It don't matter what your reasons were for nearly sending me and my mates to swing from the mast for mutiny. All that's behind us. You saved my life once, and I told you we wouldn't be square 'til I saved yours."

The cup slipped from my hands and clattered on the floor.

"We're square now, girlie. *And you ain't gonna say one word to anyone about anything.*" He pressed his calloused thumb against my lips. "'Cause the next time around, Barometer Piet won't be saving you. You got that?"

I parted my lips to speak, but Piet pressed his thumb harder. "Not. One. Word."

He left and I raced to lock the door behind him. I leaned my forehead against the rough wood and felt as though my heart would beat its way out of my chest. How long would it take for word to spread among the mutineers? How many men were waiting to take my life if I stepped outside this cabin?

Footsteps approached. The latch rattled.

"Jochims. The door, if you wouldn't mind troubling yourself."

Clockert.

Did he know? If the first mate could be part of the treachery, could the surgeon as well?

I opened the door just enough for Clockert to enter. He

looked at me quizzically and then narrowed his eyes at the marks I knew must be on my neck.

"What has gone on here?" he demanded.

"Nothing, sir," I said, nearly gagging on the lie. "Absolutely nothing."

42

Bram

"Sit down, Broen."

'Twasn't easy following De Ridder's order with Oak sprawled in front of the chair like a bear rug that's not quite dead yet. I managed by stepping over him and falling on the seat, but that left my feet in the air and nowhere to put 'em.

"Oak, roll," said the captain.

Oak snorted and rolled onto his back, leaving a few inches for me to stuff my feet under his rump.

That dog was heavy. And hot.

De Ridder'd called me to his cabin without telling me why. Now he eyed me from across his desk like he meant to take the measure of me. I tried to sit up straighter but 'twas hard with my feet stuck under his dog.

"Your father came to see me shortly before the battle with the *Lusca*. Did he tell you that?"

"No, sir." But if Pa didn't tell me, it meant what he heard from De Ridder wasn't good.

"He asked if I would consider writing a letter on your behalf to the authorities in Amsterdam, a letter of support for the petition your father filed for a certificate of legitimacy."

"Yes, sir. I know about the certificate." My face burned. Nothing like hearing your captain say out loud that he knows you're a bastard.

"I told him no."

I'd thought that spark of hope was dead in me, but it turned out it wasn't, 'cause I felt it get snuffed right there in De Ridder's office. *I told him no.*

"I'd taken note of how hard you'd been working. It was impossible not to see the long hours you kept, the extra jobs you took on, the assistance you gave to crew who had no right to expect it of you. I was impressed, Broen, and if Paulus had come to me a month earlier I should have agreed forthwith. I held your father in great esteem. I want you to know that."

So what changed his mind? What hap—*Petra*.

As if he could see inside my head De Ridder said, "And then Albert Jochims came out of the woodwork. You should know that I suspected your involvement from the first. I saw you on deck after the keelhauling, wet from the sea. Mind you, I didn't object to your helping Albert. The last thing I wanted was to see a twelve-year-old child seriously injured. But upon reflection, I realized that a twelve-year-old child would have needed help hiding on a ship with three hundred men for three months. And after that I began to wonder how you managed to make all that oakum."

What could I say? There was no denying the truth. "I'm sorry, Captain. It's all for nothing now, though, with Pa being gone."

"Actually, no, it isn't. The life of the petition extends beyond the life of the person who files it."

"Beg your pardon?"

"Just because your father died doesn't mean the authorities won't consider your claim." De Ridder opened a drawer and took out an envelope, which he slid across the desk to me. "Go ahead. Open it."

I did. Inside was a letter.

"Can you read, Broen?"

"No, Captain."

"Then you shall take my word for it that what you hold in your hand is the letter of reference I told your father I would not write."

I could still get my certificate *and* De Ridder was going to help me do it?

"I don't understand, sir."

"Don't you? As you well know, Albert Jochims is Petra De Winter, a lone girl on a ship of men. Offering her your protection was the only honorable course of action you could take, and attempting to keep her presence unknown was in her best interest. Indeed, your idea to disguise her as a boy in the event that she was discovered was a stroke of intelligence I cannot fail to admire."

I felt lower than a dog. The noble cove De Ridder wrote the letter for surely wasn't me. I stowed Petra for her sewing, not to protect her. And 'twas her idea to dress like a boy, not mine. But there was De Ridder, looking proud of me. And here I was, holding out on him.

He was the decent one, not me. And any day now he was going to have a mutiny on his hands.

⁓

After De Ridder dismissed me, I wrapped the letter in tar cloth to keep it watertight and stowed it in a pocket inside my jacket. Then I picked up Petra's rations from the galley and brought 'em to her in the sick bay. Clockert sat at his desk with an open book and a plate of toasted cheese. Petra was hunched over the worktable, ripping muslin into bandages. Her hands shook so bad she could hardly tear the flimsy stuff.

"Peas and salt pork again," I said.

Petra looked up. She was red-eyed and there was bruises on her neck.

"What the—"

She shook her head. I clenched my teeth. *Tell me.* She cast an eye at Clockert. *Later.*

Clockert stood. "I seem to have forgotten a possession of mine in another part of the ship. If you'll excuse me." He left.

I reached a hand toward Petra's shoulder but she swatted it away.

"Don't," she said, her voice like coarse sand on wood.

"Who did this?"

She shrugged.

"Gos?"

She shook her head.

"Van Assendorp?"

"No. Please, Bram, leave it."

"Miss Petra, we've had no secrets between us. Let's not start now."

She seemed small. Smaller than she was at breakfast. Smaller than she was when she had the fever. Smaller than the night we met.

"Van Plaes."

"The first mate?"

"You didn't know?" she asked.

"I would've told you if I did, wouldn't I?"

I sat down across from her at the table and she explained what happened, starting with her cod-headed idea to use Van Plaes to send a message to the captain.

I thought I knew all about the mutineers, but I missed their leader. *Idiot.* The captain's protection didn't count for much when his first mate was against him. And without Barometer Piet on her side, Petra's life was in danger above and below decks.

"You can't leave this cabin. Not ever. Not 'til we get to Java," I said.

"I know." Petra grabbed my wrist. "But if they do manage to get away, you must go with them. How many islands are there? Hundreds? Thousands? Pick one and get lost there."

It sounded good, I had to admit. Find an island—an island that looked like home but without another soul on it. No one to ask who my pa was or judge me by the color of my skin. I wouldn't be a *mestizo* anymore. I'd just be plain Bram Broen.

"You must go with them," Petra said again. "It's the only way open to you."

I'd told her what I'd learned about the mutineers, and about Jaya and Lobo, in dribs and drabs whenever we'd had time alone. Now I told her about De Ridder's letter.

"I made my choice, Miss Petra. I can't go. I'm with the captain."

43

Petra

Midshipman Majoor appeared in the sick bay the next evening. I shrank back in my chair while Clockert stood to receive the young officer.

"Good evening, sir. How can I be of service? You wouldn't be wanting a shave, would you?"

Majoor rubbed his hairless chin. "No, thank you, Master Clockert. Mister Van Plaes asked me to deliver a message. He said Jochims is to move his quarters to the orlop to berth with the other ordinary seamen."

A cry escaped me. It was an execution order.

"The boy is here at my invitation," Clockert said.

"Yes, well, Mister Van Plaes wants him to move. Tonight."

Clockert put his hand on my shoulder. "I prefer the boy to remain here. I may have need of him."

"Mister Van Plaes said you might object. He said to tell you it's the captain that wishes him moved."

Van Plaes was almost certainly lying, and Majoor was only a messenger, but without proof, Clockert couldn't call him out on it, and the captain wouldn't want to involve himself in a petty argument between a trusted officer and a troublesome girl.

"I see," Clockert said.

Majoor must have known of the hatred the men bore for me. He could sense something was amiss. He looked awkwardly around the cabin. "Right, then. I, uh, I'll be off." He hurried out.

Clockert eyed me seriously. "I assume this change of quarters has to do with more than just your sex."

"Yes, master."

"I would warn you to stay as far from this matter with the VOC payroll as possible, as I myself have done, but I can see it's too late for that."

"Very much too late," I said.

I'd no choice. I stood and began to collect my few belongings.

"Wait," Clockert said.

I looked up at the surgeon's tired face.

"It is a terrible thing to be without resources," he said in a quiet voice. "To be without family, without fortune, and, most of all, to lose one's good name. Like you, Jochims, I come from a family of means. Give me some credit," he said, holding up his hand when he saw I was about to interrupt him, "a girl does not speak as you do, does not read and write in two languages as you do, unless she comes from considerable wealth. In my case, my family were spice merchants. My grandfather was a member of government. My father was surgeon general of Holland. While my brothers prepared for a life in trade, I was to succeed my father in medicine. That is, until he ruined us through personal scandals I'm still too mortified to detail for you.

"I received news of his imprisonment and then my eldest brother's suicide while I was at university. Less than a year ago. I'm twenty-one years old—does that surprise you?"

It did. Clockert's pallid face bore no lines, his lank hair showed no gray, but his eyes were weary beyond his age.

Clockert continued without waiting for an answer. "We were left penniless. My background and unfinished education had prepared me for few areas of employment, and I was too ashamed of my family to return home. I told myself the best I could do for my mother was to find a way to eke out a living and send her my meager earnings. And so I went to sea.

"I've shared this sordid tale with no one. I share it with you now so that at least you will know there's a kindred spirit on board. One who regards you not according to your circumstances or by the actions you have been forced to take, but by the quality of the character you've displayed, which in your case is considerable."

For a moment, I was too overcome to reply. I swallowed hard. "Thank you, master. You honor me with your confidence, and your good opinion of me is a great comfort."

"I'm glad of it." Before I could say anything else, Clockert sat down at his desk. "I shall expect you at six bells tomorrow morning."

"Yes, sir."

It took only moments to finish gathering my things. I slung my ditty bag over my shoulder and headed for the crew's quarters.

I remembered the first time I'd seen this cabin, the night I stowed away. Nearly all the men had gone ashore and only Krause was there snoring off his drink. Now bodies filled hammocks in every corner and between the great guns that lined the hull.

O'Brian—an empty sleeve dangling from the shoulder where his arm used to be—spotted me in the doorway and whistled. The other sailors looked up, and a heavy silence fell. I spied the only free spot—the loudest, roughest, wettest place in the cabin—at the bow end against the outside wall. Moving my way among hostile men, my hard shoes echoed on the wood floor. When I reached up to hang my hammock, there was a rush of air by my head and a short knife twanged in the wall beside the hook.

The breath left my body. Slowly I turned around.

"Target practice," said a sailor with a gap-toothed grin.

And so it began.

～

While we sped toward the Indies, a sailor lost his lucky monkey knot. A filthy, frayed old thing, the lump of rope had been with him from his first journey as a boy and through every battle, storm, and sea thereafter. I knew this sailor. I'd held his hand while he cried over the death of his best mate during the fever. I tried to point out the hole in the corner of his ditty bag, but he wouldn't listen. The mutters and dark looks from the men told me that even if some of them believed I didn't steal the sailor's knot outright, my presence was the reason it went missing.

"Women and cats on board is considered bad luck," Bram explained. At least now I understood why the crew put up with all the rats.

I blundered badly when I noticed Louis Cheval scratching his head.

"I washed it in the piss barrel three times!" he said.

"Would you like me to cut it for you?" I offered.

"Don't say that, *Mademoiselle* Al! Do you not know the rule 'Cut neither hair nor nails at sea'?"

When a sailor fell down a hatch and split open his forehead, no one noticed he was drunk. They only saw me standing at the bottom of the ladder.

"Back off, mates," Bram said, coming between me and the glowering group.

"You back off, Broen," warned O'Brian. "Don't know why you're always hanging around this little trickster."

"Was it a trick when she took your arm off to save your life? You might show some thanks," Bram said.

"Show thanks to a snitcher? Besides, it was Clockert who took the arm off, not her. And the bad luck she brought us is probably why the gun broke off in the first place!"

True, Clockert had wielded the saw, but I'd done the stitching up after and held O'Brian's head when he cried upon waking. But nothing Bram said or did made a difference, except to direct some of the crew's dark looks at him as well as me. The crew were none too fond of him for taking my side, but unlike me, Bram had some protection: his maleness and the crew's respect for Paulus.

Even the soldiers wanted nothing to do with me. I made sure never to move around the ship alone for fear of being thrown overboard. I especially avoided Van Plaes.

I had another concern as well—being the only female aboard a ship of men who hadn't had feminine companionship for months. Bram moved his hammock from the carpenter's cabin and slung it next to mine so I would have the wall on one side and him on the other when I slept. But he couldn't prevent every curse and elbow. When I lifted my shirt in the privacy of the empty infirmary, my torso was a patchwork of purple, yellow, and green.

"I guess I don't need these anymore, Tina," I whispered, unwinding the linen wraps I'd been wearing for so long. I kept on my male clothes, as I had no others.

Oddly, Happy Jan was kind. He gave me an extra helping of salted penguin and stared down the sailor who started to object. When he spooned the food into my bowl I noticed a fresh burn running the length of one forearm.

"That must hurt quite a bit," I said.

Happy Jan looked startled, which made him seem only a trifle less fierce than usual. Few people ever spoke to him directly.

"Could be worse," he said.

"Would you . . . What I mean to say is, I could bind it for you and give you some willow bark for the pain. If . . . if you wish."

Happy Jan considered my offer, and I tried not to stare at the rows of scars on his face. While he thought, he pressed his lips together and I couldn't see his pointed teeth, a mercy I appreciated. At last he said, "Thank you. I would like that."

I hurried to the sick bay for supplies and was back in minutes. Happy Jan left his mate to dole out dinner and we went up to the bow. He sat on one of the privy boxes while I assembled my medicines.

"How did you do it?" I asked, applying honey as gently as I could. "Taking a pan from the oven?"

"Aye," he said. "How did you know?"

"There was a boy I knew in Amsterdam, a baker's boy. He could never remember to wear a mitt and so came to us every week with burns like yours."

"Us? You were doctor's assistant?"

"No, not a doctor, my—" I stumbled over my words, so accustomed was I to lying about my past and who I was.

"You don't have to answer," Happy Jan said. "We all have stories we don't want to share."

We were both silent while I wrapped Happy Jan's arm in a clean bandage. I could only imagine the stories Happy Jan wouldn't wish to share after selling his own people into slavery.

"Thank you," he said when I finished. "It feels better."

"Happy Jan," I said. "You know something of my troubles on the ship, I think. Most of the men despise me. Why are you so kind?"

All the air seemed to leave him then. Huge Happy Jan shriveled before my eyes. Hunched over on the stool, he rubbed his hands on his knees over and again.

"I have much to atone for."

Bram

I was on my way to eat breakfast with Petra in the sick bay when Jaya found me.

"We move tomorrow night, my brother."

The ocean lurched and rolled. Me and Jaya had to steady ourselves against the walls of the companionway.

"Already?" I asked.

"You want to wait more? You mad, brother?"

"No, it's just—"

Jaya cut me off. "You know, others, they say to me, Jaya, why do you trust Bram Broen? He is all the time with Albert, and Albert, she listens into doors and speaks when she shouldn't speak. I say to them, no, no, Bram is good boy. He has good good heart like his father and he feel sorry for little girl. Tell me, Bram, am I right? Because if I am not right, then we have big big problem."

Thunder growled in the distance.

"Aye, you're right, *Om*." I met his eye. "I feel sorry for her is all."

"Good," Jaya said. "You make sure you are ready, yes? Tomorrow night."

"Aye," I said.

44

Petra

"All hands hoay! All hands hoay!"

The bosun's call to the deck at this hour of the after-noon was unexpected and irregular. Clockert rose from his desk without bothering to close his books.

The trumpet sounded and the bosun called again.

"All hands hoay!"

"Come, Jochims," Clockert said.

I hung up the glister syringe I'd been cleaning and fol-lowed the doctor to the fo'c'sle. The madness that had been brewing was coming to a head. I could feel it. The air thrummed with the drumbeat of hundreds of feet march-ing upward from the lower decks toward we knew not what. Not one voice spoke.

Outside, the *Lion* was stalled head to wind. The soldiers were locked below, but all the sailors were assembled. They hung from the rigging and crowded the decks, except for a clearing in the waist where Happy Jan had been butchering a sow. The beast easily weighed three hundred pounds. It lay, headless and gutless, on a table made of six long boards fixed together in a square set loose on top of two trestles. Happy Jan was stowing a large cleaver and several other knives in a sack, his hands shiny with pig blood.

Master Clockert and I found a place in a corner of the fo'c'sle near the bow. I scanned the crowds and found Lobo perched amidships on a rail with an arm around Louis. Bram pushed his way through the crowds to stand beside me, looking as grim as I felt.

"What's happening?" I whispered.

"Over there," he said, pointing with his chin.

De Ridder and Van Plaes commanded the quarterdeck with Oak behind them. Between the officers was Van Assendorp. In irons. He'd a cuff around his neck and manacles on his wrists and ankles, all connected by a long chain that ran from top to bottom. One of Van Assendorp's eyes was swollen shut, and there was blood spattered on his shirt. Van Plaes held the free end of the chain like a leash, his lipless mouth curled down in disgust.

"Men!" the captain shouted. "I've called you to witness the accusation and imprisonment of Diederick Van

Assendorp, commander of soldiers, for the most serious crime on any ship. *Mutiny*."

A murmur went through the crowd. But not a gasp. By now the plot was secret to no one.

"Mister Van Assendorp has designed to steal cargo from the Dutch East India Company ship *Golden Lion*. He has corrupted and conspired with men under his command to usurp my authority as captain."

Only then did I see the others in irons near the quarterdeck rail. Jaya, Barometer Piet, Kosnik, Gos, and Goth.

"Bram," I whispered. "How did the captain—?"

"I told him," he whispered back. "In his cabin. After he gave me the letter."

"Did you tell him about Van Plaes?"

"I didn't know about Van Plaes then."

Van Plaes held Van Assendorp's chain tightly with both hands. I surmised his bruised knuckles had something to do with Van Assendorp's swollen eye and the blood on his shirt.

"You don't think—?" I asked.

"What?"

"Look at Van Plaes's hands," I whispered. "He's beaten Van Assendorp raw. Could he have been putting on a show and been the captain's man on the inside all along?"

"What about what he did to you in Clockert's cabin?"

"Part of the show, perhaps?"

"That didn't look like a show," Bram said.

"Then what's he up to now?"

"Shhh," Clockert warned us.

"Mister Van Assendorp," commanded the captain, a mixture of fury and disgust deepening the lines on his face, "have you anything to say on your own behalf?"

All shuffles and whispers ceased. Van Assendorp's red face deepened to wine, his white scar like a scythe on his cheek.

"No," he said.

"As you say. Your crime is indefensible." Turning to the crew, De Ridder asked, "Is there any man here who wishes to speak for Mister Van Assendorp before he is imprisoned in the hold with his fellow conspirators, there to remain until they can be tried and sentenced in Batavia?"

A long silence followed, during which no one dared move.

"Mister Van Plaes—"

"Captain!" Van Plaes interrupted. "There is something I wish to say."

"Please do," De Ridder said, looking surprised but not alarmed.

"I'm sorry."

"I beg your pardon?"

"It wasn't intended to end like this."

Van Plaes pulled a pistol from his jacket and fired. De Ridder slumped to the deck. The crowd erupted. Oak snarled and leaped for Van Plaes's neck.

Bodies struggled—to fight the mutineers, to join them, to flee—but packed together, no one was free to move. From below came the rumble of soldiers shouting and pounding the decks. I was crushed against the rail, knocked by flailing arms and legs until Bram shoved me between Clockert and himself.

On the quarterdeck Van Assendorp and the others had thrown off their chains. Now they were passing around muskets, retrieved from a hiding place under a tarp on the quarterdeck.

A gunshot fired into the air startled the ship into something like quiet. Van Plaes stood in the captain's usual place at the center of the quarterdeck, a smoking pistol in one hand and a bloody handkerchief pressed to his jaw with the other. He could thank Oak for that wound, poor Oak, who was now leashed a few feet away, howling over his dead master's body.

"Lions! Avast ye!" he commanded. The crew eyed him warily. "I have command of this ship now, and all who choose to follow me shall be rewarded for their loyalty. Ask yourselves this: What light purse did you expect to receive for your nine months' hard labor on this ship? Join me now, and I shall double it. Nay, triple it!"

The appeal of Van Plaes's offer was marred somewhat by Oak's whines and the red pool around De Ridder.

"And if we don't?" shouted a voice from the starboard rigging.

"Those of you who are with my men and me shall go about your duties as usual until we make land, whereupon you shall be given your fair share of the VOC payroll, and we shall part as comrades," Van Plaes answered. "Those opposed shall berth in lock-up in the hold."

"Why should we believe you'll give us our fair share?" called another voice. "Why should we think you won't kill us like you killed De Ridder?"

Van Plaes pressed the handkerchief harder against his cheek. "No one is more grieved than I by the death of Captain De Ridder. It was brought about by the loose tongue of one of this company. I assure you, gentlemen, that loose tongue will be silenced."

An oily fear trickled down my spine. Next to me, Bram drew in a sharp breath.

"Now then, if there are no further questions . . ." Van Plaes surveyed the decks. "Who is with me?"

Most hands went up. But not mine, and not Bram's.

Van Plaes's men began rounding up the people who couldn't deny being De Ridder's supporters, like Slippert, whose allegiance to the captain was well-known. Most gave in without a fight. Against the firearms of the mutineers, what hope had they of resistance? It was only a matter of time before they came to Bram and me, and we'd nowhere to hide.

The mutineers pressed ahead to the waist, shackling the few who tried to defy them. But almost everyone claimed to be with Van Plaes. When the mutineers reached Happy Jan, he pulled a machete from his sack and held it out in front of him, swinging it slowly from side to side.

"I belong to no man," he said.

The mutineers looked to their leader.

"Leave him be," Van Plaes said.

The mutineers were at the fo'c'sle now, just a few feet away. The soldiers were shouting and pounding again.

"You," Van Plaes said, raising his voice to be heard over the soldiers and pointing at a crewman I knew only by sight. "You're the son of De Ridder's housemaid."

"Not on my life, sir—"

"Don't deny it." Van Plaes adjusted the wadded cloth on his cheek and winced. "I have the ship's log."

Barometer Piet held out a rope. "Over here, mate. No use fighting it. You'll be safe enough in the hold."

The young man twisted through the crowd and allowed Piet to tie his hands. Van Plaes repeated this process with two other sailors until, finally, his eye landed on Bram and me. My stomach turned to ice. I found Bram's hand and gripped it hard.

"Ah! Mister Broen and Miss De Winter. The source of all our trouble today. Were it not for the bad luck Miss De Winter brought upon us and Mister Broen's whispers in the captain's ear, we should have avoided this bloodshed altogether."

Looking around, I saw a great deal of nodding and narrowing of eyes, even among the men who were tied up. Bram and I had few friends on the ship. We'd find no help here.

"Were it not for you two," Van Plaes continued, "Captain De Ridder would still be among us, Mister Van Assendorp would have been spared humiliation, and I would still have my left cheek!"

Van Plaes dropped the handkerchief with a flourish and a chorus of cries went around at the sight of the terrible wound Oak had given him. Every word he spoke must have been excruciating.

Van Plaes wanted blood for blood. And the blood he wanted was ours.

The soldiers thundered louder. I could feel their pounding through the deck.

"Broen! De Winter! Come here!"

Perhaps a dozen crew separated us from our fate. I locked eyes with Bram. He knew as well as I what would happen if we crossed that space: Death. Quick or slow, but certain all the same.

Clockert put his hands on our shoulders. "Leave them, Van Plaes. They're children," he said.

"They're grown enough to lie, steal, and spy, Master Clockert!" Van Plaes's voice rose and he was sweating. I'd seen this side of him in Clockert's cabin when he nearly strangled me. "If they're grown enough to be keelhauled, they're grown enough for what I have in mind for them.

Come to think of it, Mister Broen will fetch a good price in the Batavia slave market. Perhaps I shan't be too rough with him after all."

Bram squeezed my hand hard enough to break bone.

"Come, my brother," Jaya called, holding out a rope. "It is better if you do not fight."

"As for Miss De Winter, shall I ransom her to her father or sell her to the highest bidder along with her friend here?"

Better death than that.

We were at the far end of the fo'c'sle with no way out except toward Van Plaes and his men. Clockert had tried to help us, but what could he do against so many? I looked for a friendly face. Louis was weeping with his face buried in Lobo's shirt. Lobo himself was staring at Bram and me but not with hatred. I glanced down at Happy Jan in the waist, and his eyes spoke a message, though I couldn't say what.

I turned to Bram. Was slavery our fate? Had I traded my father in Amsterdam for Van Plaes here at sea?

The sea.

It surrounded us, sunlight crackling the green waves. Without question there was death in those waters. Death by drowning, death by sharks. But also freedom and the peace of a death by choice. And, just perhaps, a slim hope of survival.

I cocked my head at Bram. *Yes?* The corners of his mouth turned up. *Yes.*

I looked down at Happy Jan again, this time with understanding. He nodded and gripped the edge of the table.

"Fare thee well, master," I whispered to Clockert.

As one, Bram and I jumped the rail and leaped into the ocean, just as Happy Jan flipped the great sow onto the deck and hurled the tabletop after us.

Cold water stole my breath but only for a moment. I climbed onto Bram's back and he swam for the tabletop, now a makeshift raft that was our only chance of survival.

Shouts of anger rained down on us, but over them rang a few cries of triumph.

"Clap on, Miss Petra," Bram said when we reached the raft.

I slithered on and pulled Bram up after me, then turned for one last glimpse of the *Lion* in time to see Van Plaes's infuriated face and Lobo's and Louis's joyful ones. Barometer Piet turned his back, and Clockert tipped his hat at us with a rare smile. Jaya spat red betel juice into the sea, and Happy Jan pressed his palms together and raised them over his head. We paddled madly away. A few gunshots followed, but at this distance they went wild. Before long, we'd lost sight of the ship.

Bram and I were alone in the vast Indian Ocean.

Epilogue

Bram

I cracked open my eyes. The raft was still rocking, but the boards was soft and lumpy, and the masts'd grown leaves.

Leaves?

Not the ocean then. Or the *Lion*. Something else. Somewhere else. Overhead, three trees, not three masts. The biggest trees I'd ever seen, maybe a hundred feet tall.

No, not three trees. Just one. A man's length from the ground, they fed into one thick trunk, bigger around than my granny's house.

That tree must've been growing for a thousand years.

I was too stoved up to sit, so I stayed where I was, looking at the tree but seeing the ocean, the *Lion*, Petra.

Petra.

She lay on the beach next to me. Asleep, not dead. I knew she was alive because I still had a grip on her wrist, and she mine, and I could feel her pulse.

I tried to let go. Nothing doing. Though even if I could pry my fingers off her flesh, I expected they'd stay curled like claws forever, because nothing would ever matter more than holding on. Didn't matter how cold the water was or how hot the sun, or how hungry or thirsty I was, or how many sharks circled us.

Nothing would ever matter more than holding fast to Petra's wrist.

I listened to the waves wash the shore. How long was we adrift? Two days? Three?

Hang on . . . was I dead?

No. I was too sore and thirsty to be in heaven and not sore and thirsty enough to be in hell.

We'd paddled for a while, and then, when we ran out of strength, we let the current carry us. We hardly spoke, 'cept every now and again to keep Petra's spirits up I'd say something like, "I bet we find land before nightfall," or to keep mine up, she'd say, "At least our clothes will be clean after this." The first night we sang songs in the dark to keep from being scared. Every shanty we knew, songs our mothers taught us, and songs we made up. Like this one: "A boy and a girl set sail on a lark; they sailed in the day and they sailed in the dark; they hoped they'd not get eaten by a shark; oh, where's that Noah with his great big ark; what's that I see, hoay there, hark! Hell's bells, it's a . . ." Then we pretended to choke and die.

Singing helped until the second day, when our throats was so parched we could hardly make a sound. With no hat, Petra's skin was burnt crisp by midmorning. I offered her my shirt for cover, but she was too pigheaded to take it.

When the sharks found us, 'twas no less than what we expected. Me and Petra shifted nearer each other and pressed our foreheads together. We curled our legs out of the water and waited.

"It'll be quick," I said.

"It was bound to happen one way or another," she said.

But more fins came, bigger ones on shiny backs. The dolphins chased the sharks away. Then they showed off for us, one crew jumping and diving while another crew pushed the raft. Petra and me, we screamed for joy, dry throats be damned. The rush of the water and the panting of the dolphins through their blowholes was better than any music.

Around nightfall, the dolphins swam off, and we was alone and adrift again. That was the bleakest time of all. Cold, burnt, parched, and hopeless, I cried with my face turned so Petra wouldn't see me. When the tears ran out, I fought off pictures in my head of bloody decks and angry faces 'til sleep took me and I saw worse in my nightmares.

"That's the tallest tree I've ever seen."

Petra was awake and staring up, eyes swollen in her blistered face, brows and lashes bleached near white, lips cracked and oozing.

"And the widest," I agreed.

"Are we dead?"

"Don't think so."

"No, I don't think so either."

We watched the leaves shift in the light breeze.

"Any idea where?" she asked.

"None at all."

"Nor I."

The bark was smooth and shiny. Silver.

"Are you thirsty?" Petra coughed weakly.

"Just a bit."

Our throats was too dry to laugh. Using one hand each, we pushed ourselves up to sit and then stared at our wrists.

"Guess we don't need to hold on anymore," I said.

We tried to let go, but our fingers wouldn't move. Finally Petra wrapped her free hand around my frozen one.

"This will hurt."

I set my teeth. She tried to be gentle, but even so 'twas like breaking bone. When Petra'd made a little space, she went to work on her own hand, prying open her fingers just enough so's we could slip apart.

"Ready to go find some water?" I asked, rubbing my knuckles.

Petra nodded. If she was like me, it hurt to talk.

We'd washed up on a beach. White powder sand, a calm blue sea. Sea grass lined the shore maybe twenty yards from the water line. Beyond the grass was dense jungle. A ways away a mountain puffed up clouds of gray smoke.

We stumbled away from the shore and into the trees, swaying like people who'd been too long on the water with too little to eat. 'Twas plenty warm out, so I couldn't understand why I was shivering. Petra was shivering too. She caught me looking at her. "An excess of cold moist humors causes body tremors. We were overlong in the water."

I grunted in answer.

"I don't know how to find fresh water," she said.

"Look for animal tracks. Follow birds."

I went ahead, but my legs wouldn't hold me. I staggered and grabbed hold of a vine.

"Are you all right?"

I steadied myself and forced a smile. "Just need to get my land legs."

We wobbled in a general direction away from the beach, stopping every so often for me to check a broken twig or a chewed leaf. Long vines twisted around tree trunks like wads of brown paper wrung out and left to dry. Little pink flowers trailed over moss beds and waxy white ones hung from trees.

Before long we found a big rock with puddles of rainwater on its face. Without shame we leaned in, one to a puddle, and lapped up the water like dogs. When we'd drunk it all, we slid onto the ground and rested our backs against the rock.

"That's a start," I said.

"We'll rest just a moment and then go find more," Petra said.

But we rested longer than a moment. We woke hours later, when the sky that'd been cloudless all morning dumped barrels of rain on us. We turned up our faces and stretched out our arms and let the water pour down our throats and wash away the salt. Swift as it started, the rain stopped and the sky brightened up like nothing had happened.

"Look," Petra said.

"What?"

"We're still wearing them."

Of all things, my belt was still on me—with most of the tools still in it. Petra had on her medicine belt too, and her short knife. I checked my jacket pocket. De Ridder's letter was there, dry in its wrappings.

"Sink me," I said.

We set off again, a little steadier now, and found a stream with good fresh water. We took our time sipping.

I stood and stretched my back, while Petra sat on a rock with her face tipped to the sky. There was no sign of life anywhere except for us and the birds.

"That's better," I said.

"Hmm."

"Miss Petra?"

"Hmm?"

"What d'you suppose we should do now?"

She sighed and pushed herself up to stand. "You're right, of course. We should get started gathering food and firewood and building a shelter while we wait for a ship to pick us up."

I squinted at the sun winking off dark green leaves and smelled all those little white flowers.

"Or?" I said.

"Or?" she said.

"Or maybe we don't wait for a ship to pick us up," I said. "Maybe we stay here awhile."

We both thought about that. Pictured us two here on this island. Not a mixed-race boy and a lone girl, but just us. Bram and Petra.

"There'd be plenty of fish for eating," I said.

"Coconuts too," Petra said, seeing it with me, "and likely more fruits as well."

"Palm leaves would make for a good thatch roof, and with the tools I got left, I could build us something like a house. Or at least a lean-to. And when we got a fire going and our shelter built—"

"And some food stored—"

"What then, Miss Petra? Think of it!"

What then?

Author's Note

There's a well-known adage that you should write what you know. I'd like to add a corollary: It's okay to write what you don't know; just make sure you do a lot of research.

A lot of research.

I had this great idea for a book about two kids who sail from Amsterdam to the East Indies in the seventeenth century. My only problem was that all I knew about the seventeenth century was that it was the same thing as the 1600s. Also, I was unclear about the whole Holland versus Netherlands thing. And I was rusty on humoral theory.

No matter. I like a challenge. I researched for a full year before I started writing, and after I started writing, I kept researching. I'm still researching. (I like researching.)

Today my *Cast Off* file has almost four hundred different source notes (for a selected bibliography, please visit my website, www.eveyohalem.com). I read lots of books: scholarly academic stuff, journalistic stuff, fiction, memoirs, journals, every first-person account I could find. I spoke to people who knew much more than I—VOC scholars, maritime scholars, curators, my husband (he sails), surgeons, and dentists. I hung out in oddball museums. I traveled to Indonesia, where I slept in the jungle and held baby orangutans, and to the Netherlands, where I retraced every step of Petra's that I could and explored the dark nooks of two different full-scale East Indiamen replicas.

(For the record, I'm a terrible sailor. My husband has tried hard to teach me, but every time he starts to talk about wind and heading up or heading down, I get tired. But I've spent a fair amount of time on boats, and there was this one night a long time ago where I clung to the jib of a thirty-foot sailboat, searching for an unfamiliar harbor in a teeming rainstorm. For the purposes of this novel, I extrapolated.)

I have no research training. It would have helped if I'd majored in history in college, but I didn't. Mostly, I followed my nose. I knew that my story would begin in Amsterdam and take place mostly at sea on an East Indiaman bound for Batavia. I knew two of my characters: a Dutch girl and an East Indian boy, both twelve years old. That's a lot to get started with.

What's surgery like by candlelight below deck on a rocking ship before the invention of anesthesia? How do you fire a four-thousand-pound cannon without getting crushed by the recoil? These were the kinds of questions I tried to answer.

Details about housekeeping, clothing, décor, Dutch fastidiousness (fanatical about their homes, not so much about their bodies), food, and medicine are all authentic. Whether the streets were brick or dirt, the ten p.m. curfew—all true in 1660s Amsterdam.

I tried to convey what it felt like to cram three hundred men onto a 150-foot-long vessel for six months (damp, dark, and airless below, smelled bad, no privacy). The layout of the *Golden Lion* is based on actual ships of the period, as are the various jobs, daily schedule, terrible food. The three-million-florin payroll that got shipped to Batavia twice a year in lead-bound trunks? True.

And there really were laws preventing mixed-race children

of Dutch fathers and East Indian mothers from setting foot on Dutch soil, and similar laws preventing Dutch females from going to East India.

All of the characters are fictional, with the exception of Pieter and Eva Van Meerhof. There really was a white European doctor married to a black Khoikhoi woman in Dutch Cape Town in the 1660s (although the real Pieter Van Meerhof was Danish, not Dutch). It was quite a scandal. The names and nationalities of all the sailors on the *Lion* were taken from an actual Dutch ship's log of the period, but I made up the personalities to go with them.

For Petra's and Doctor Clockert's medical knowledge, I have to thank John Woodall's *The Surgeon's Mate,* a seventeenth-century medical guide no ship's surgeon would have been without.

I tried really hard to get the details right, but I'm sure I made plenty of mistakes, and I take full responsibility for all of them (even though I would prefer to blame other people). Also, this seems like the right place to confess that sometimes I fudged the truth to serve my story. For example, the *Lion* would have been part of a fleet, and she wouldn't have sailed from the Amsterdam harbor because it wasn't deep enough to accommodate such a big ship. Also, Clockert's office would have been much smaller. But the really gross stuff in the book—like wormy water and butt-brooms—is all accurate, because I care deeply about things like that.

Eve Yohalem, New York, August 2014

Acknowledgments

Writing *Cast Off* was, as they say in transoceanic shipping, a long haul, and I had a lot of help along the way. Ginger Knowlton, my wonderful agent, of the many moments I've cherished with you, my favorite may be when I asked why you thought you'd be able to sell a novel of seventeenth-century historical fiction, and you said, "Why wouldn't I?" Emma Dryden, there were times in this journey when all that kept me going was the mantra "Emma doesn't think I'm crazy."

Thank you, marvelous editors Liz Waniewski and Kate Harrison, for inviting me to join the Dial family and making me feel at home. *Cast Off* is a way better book as a result of your gentle yet laser-sharp queries. Thanks, too, to the rest of the Dial team.

Deep appreciation to my keen-eyed readers Amelia Dalvito, Theodore Strauss, and Julie Sternberg. Many thanks to my meticulous research assistants Ian Delaney and Pippi Kessler. Jeffrey Stock, everything I know about Indonesian languages I learned from you.

Fellow author Mina Witteman, VOC scholar Dirk Tang, and Ernst van Keulen of the National Maritime Museum in Amsterdam, your generous gifts of time and knowledge have enriched me and this book.

Marc Acito, last time you held my hand up the mountain. This time you strapped me to your back and hoisted me up. Nick, Joe, and Maya, you are the best part of every day.

Thank you for *everything*: your advice, enthusiasm, insights, reality checks, and good humor—and especially for liking all the gross parts as much as I do.

Finally, love and gratitude to Jack Aubrey and Stephen Maturin, who instilled in me a passion for sea adventures.